Enjoy the Kw

Kymber
Morgan

Praise for Kymber Morgan

Ms Morgan is a fabulous new voice. If you are a fan of romantic comedy, with the imaginative use of Greek mythology woven in, you'll love SHAFTED. ~ *BMC "Book Babe"*

SHAFTED is a fast-paced story packed with everything we love about paranormal romance. A great mix of sarcasm and wit that left me laughing to the very last sentence. ~ *ZodiacBookReviews*

I don't want to give away any plot twists or turns because they are so fun to watch as you read. A hilarious ride with the Gods of Olympia. Give SHAFTED a try, you won't regret it
~ *The Delighted Reader*

SHAFTED - A fast paced story by a talented author. I can hardly wait for the next installment.
~ *My Book Addiction and More*

Kymber Morgan delivers a meaty story that brings old world mythology to the equally mythical town of Bandit Creek Montana. SHAFTED will keep you chuckling long after Cupid's arrows have hit their target. ~ *Roxy Boroughs, Author of 'A Stranger's Touch'*

Acknowledgements:

A special thanks to Roxy Boroughs, Susan Retzlaff and Victoria Chatham for putting up with the first draft and helping me take this story from there to here. To my Bro, for letting me bandy his name around in this story and for being a wonderful friend. And as always, to my husband and son for all their love and support (and for making sure I have food and water when I'm writing).

And thank you, Dear Reader, for joining Chase and Jenna on their *Wild* romantic ride.

Dedication:

This book is dedicated to the men and woman who continue to keep this piece of western heritage alive and to the families cheering their wins and supporting them through the losses no matter the challenge or heartache. My hat is off to you.

Wild for Cowboy
By
Kymber Morgan

Chapter 1

"Uh...."

"That's not exactly the response I was expecting."

Jenna Cordell stood there with her mouth hanging open and her stomach beginning to churn like someone had turned on a blender. Her Aunt hadn't really said that. Had she? Maybe Jenna needed to get her hearing checked.

It wasn't unusual for her to drop in on Jenna at work, nor was she unknown for popping little surprises on her niece, but not like this.

Before she could decide if she should kiss her aunt or flatten her, the sound of screeching tires and a long horn blast invaded the gallery. With the front door open to offset the early July heat, the barrage of off-color language that followed came in loud and clear.

"Hang on Auntie Kate." Jenna stepped around 'Marty', the life sized bronze-cast replica of a bull moose dominating the entryway and gave the heavy oak slab a shove while she tried to absorb her aunt's announcement.

She had to be dreaming. That was it. She looked out the window trying to confirm her theory.

Nope, nothing had changed. Cars still had wheels, not feet, buildings had windows, not eyes, and Sadie the bag lady still sat next to her shopping cart, not a scale model of the Titanic.

Okay she'd had some weird dreams, but what artist didn't?

Even the garish banner, stretched across the guard-rail of a nearby overpass, still showed a cowboy hat atop a black silhouette with the question: 'Are you a *'Wild'* man?' splashed below in big red letters.

Hmph. So much for the sandman explanation, any self-respecting dream would have a to-die-for man's face in place of that silhouette.

A set of twinkling green eyes, fringed in thick black lashes, flashed in her mind and Jenna instinctively shoved it away. Not that one.

Jenna glanced over her shoulder at the gallery behind her. It still showcased the same wild life and traditional western bronzes it had yesterday and none of the paintings had mysteriously morphed into modern abstract - and her aunt hadn't changed one bit.

Her head was still covered in red spikes and the rhinestone and turquoise embroidered scrollwork, running the length of her jean clad legs, hadn't slid

off into a pool around her leopard patterned
stilettos. Her matching top still wasn't doing a thing
to camouflage her double helping of feminine
attributes and she hadn't stopped chewing on her
ruby red bottom lip or fidgeting like a child busting
to tell a great secret.

Okay, not a dream, not an altered reality; that
brought her back to possible hearing problems.

Not sure if she was hoping it was her ears or
not, Jenna crossed her fingers and held her breath.
"Would you mind repeating that please?"

Auntie Kate hooked Jenna's bent elbow and
steered her back around so they faced each other.
"Oh for heaven's sake Jenna-Lynn, you heard me
well enough. I said you're one of the four-day
artists for the Western Art Showcase at this year's
Stampede." How she managed to bounce on the
balls of her feet in those heels Jenna would never
know. "Can you believe it, Jenz? The Stampede!"

Holy crap, she was serious.

Jenna's inner blender sped up to puree mode
and her knees felt weak. Could she face going back
there? Had enough time passed? *Relax, the art show
is on the opposite end of the grounds, nowhere near
the in-field.*

Even it that weren't an issue, they were talking

about the Calgary Stampede Western Art show here; one of the biggest and most prestigious around, was her work ready for something like that? And how did this happen?

"But, I can't be in, I never applied." Great, now she sounded like a broken rubber ducky.

"I know you didn't silly, because I did it for you." Kate's cheek splitting grin turned into a girlish giggle, completely at odds with her forty some years.

"You did what?" A strange buzzing noise invaded Jenna's skull.

"Since I knew you'd never do it, I talked to my friend Pattie and she got me an application. I filled it out on your behalf, fired it off, and voila."

Tiny dots crept into Jenna's vision and the room was getting stuffier by the minute. Maybe she should've left the door open. "But how could you without me signing it?" Jenna dislodged Kate's fingers and took a step back, all systems preparing for full-on panic. "Didn't they want to see a portfolio?"

Kate swung her bracelet-laden arm toward the adjoining room causing a tinkling echo through the place. "Mrs. Goreman let me in and I took pictures of the sculptures you have on display here. It was easy."

She glanced away and plucked a non-existent bit of lint from her sleeve setting off an alarm in Jenna's head.

"Well, at least it was with Pattie's help."

Pattie's help! What had they done? Pattie had been with the Stampede administration office for years. "What if she gets fired? Have you lost your mind Auntie?"

Jenna slowly sunk down onto the window sill. "There are strict rules about these things." Her ducky squeak dropped to a whisper. "What if they figure out it wasn't me who applied? What if I get kicked out half way through? What'll happen to my career? I'll never be taken seriously again."

Kate crouched down in front of her and wrapped her hands around Jenna's clenched fists. "Honey relax, as usual you worry too much. After all, it's not like you signed your name to someone else's work." Her expression took on a 'you should know better' cast. "Besides, we're not dumb, Pattie cleared everything with the board of directors before your entry went in. And besides there was an opening left after the Thursday auction they hadn't filled yet. So it's all good, okay?"

Jenna's fingers started to uncurl and her breathing slowed a bit. "So this wasn't you two bending rules or cutting corners like you sometimes do?" She leaned closer and searched her aunt's face. "I really am in on my own merit, everything's on the up and up?"

"Hmph, if I didn't love you so much I'd be insulted. Us cut corners? Try to imagine. Pattie and I are nothing if not straight as...?" Kate's brow wrinkled. "Innocent as the...?" She pursed her lips, shrugged her shoulders and winked. "Okay, maybe not. But—in this case everything is legit. All you have to do is pay the fee and show up."

"Fee?" Jenna's balloon popped and her stomach shifted from blend to nose-dive. Of course there was a fee, a show like this came with an equally prestigious price attached.

The light in her aunt's eyes dimmed. "You have some money saved up don't you? I mean, when I took the pictures, Mrs. G. said the sales on your consignment work's been picking up, and with the classes you're teaching here during the week, you can come up with the money, right?"

Kate, the forty-something bouncing toddler, looked like Jenna was about to take her candy away. Impulsive and at times borderline interfering she might be, but Jenna loved her aunt dearly and hated to see her upset about anything. She also couldn't lie her way out of a paper bag so had no idea what to say.

If the gallery wasn't closing for at least a week because of mechanical problems Jenna might've been able to pull it off. But no gallery meant no classes or sales. No classes or sales - no money. Things were already going to be tight this month and the show was less than two weeks away. Where was she going to get that kind of money on such short notice?

"Honey, you can come up with the fee can't you?"

Jenna scrambled. "Sure, yah...I think...maybe...if."

Kate's face paled, then she wobbled her way to a standing position and started to pace, tapping her chin with one long red finger nail as she did. "Okay, let's not panic here. Maybe I could cash in a bond early or something. Or talk to Pattie...see if they'd let you pay part now and part after the show."

When Jenna was old enough to understand that Kate had gone without many times so her sister's orphaned child wouldn't have to, she vowed she'd do her best to make it up to her kind-hearted aunt one day. Kate had always encouraged Jenna to follow her dreams and done everything in her power to help her do just that. No way was Jenna letting her dip into her meager savings now.

She'd simply have to find the money somehow.

Jenna pasted what she hoped resembled a smile on her face and nodded her head. "Uh, no really, it's no problem, Auntie. I'm sure I can work something out. Guess I'm still in shock is all." Jenna fanned the air in front of her face. "Whew."

With a squeal, Kate's face broke back into a grin and she clapped her hands, bringing the forty-year old toddler back. "That's my girl."

It was all Jenna could do to keep up the façade as she walked Kate out front to her car and hugged her good-bye. She watched until Kate's '73, something-or-other, tank of a car pulled away and shot over the flyover into the city's core heading for Chinatown.

She knew Kate couldn't wait to relay Jenna's reaction to their little surprise to Pattie and she shuttered to think what the next episode of the 'Mischief Twins' might entail as the two to them hatched plans over fried chicken feet and dumplings.

Lost in thought Jenna stepped back inside the

gallery coming face to snout with the Marty the bronze moose. "Ahhh!" She skirted the moose and gave it a dirty look. "Not funny Marty."

"Jenna? That you?" Her boss and owner of the gallery, Mrs. Goreman, called from the back. She flipped the sign to closed, spun the deadbolt and hit the main light switch as she pulled her purse and the daily deposit bag out of the safe. "Yes Mrs. Goreman, it's me. I was just locking up. Be right there."

In spite of several derelict warehouses turning high end condo and a plethora of trendy shops and restaurants finding homes in the vicinity, Mrs. G. kept up her late husband's practice of coming by the gallery every night at closing. She claimed it was to save the staff the trouble of taking the day's deposit to the bank, but they all knew it was because she liked the company.

Jenna came around the corner and Mrs. G. jumped, slipping something into her purse and a tinge of pink washed over her powdery cheeks. "Oh there you are dear, let me grab my key."

Was that a compact she'd dropped in there? "It's okay, I have mine." Jenna smiled as she secured the door and followed her to the parking lot. She'd never seen the elderly woman move so fast.

"What's the rush Mrs. G., hot date tonight or something?"

Five brisk steps later her cheeks had turned from pink to red and one shoulder lifted in a tiny shrug. "Since you asked. Yes."

Jenna almost tripped. She did? Mrs. Goreman had been a widow for ten years now and hadn't so much as walked beside a man to the refreshment table at church for fear of smirching Mr. Goreman's memory, let alone gone out with one.

"Okay, you can't drop a bomb like that and then go all zip-lip on me." Jenna bent down so she could see her face more clearly and grinned. "Come on now, spill. You can tell me. Who is it?"

Her employer and friend blushed even more. "Fine, Miss Snoopy McSnoop, if you must know, his name is Mr. Deagel. He's the gentleman I hired to do the maintenance on the heating system at the gallery." Her pregnant pause made it clear that was all she intended to say on the matter. "Oh, you do recall we'll be closing for the next week because of it right?"

Jenna decided to let her off the hook for now. "Yes, I remember. And nice try, but that doesn't mean I won't grill you about this interesting tidbit later." This brought her thoughts back to her own new development. "Would there be a problem if I drop by on the weekend to pick up some of my work?"

Mrs. G. reached for her car door but paused before opening it. "I don't think that should be a problem, I'll let Mr. Deagel know you're coming. What do you need the pieces for dear?"

Jenna decided before she lost her nerve and Mrs. G. drove away she'd try one of her aunt's favourite strategies - Fake it, till you make it. "Turns out I've been accepted as one of the four-day artists at this year's Stampede art show but I'll need around twenty-five to thirty items to fill the booth. Given the short time frame, I was hoping to pull some of them from the work on display at the gallery."

"Oh my, that's wonderful news." She looked at Jenna closer and squinted. "Isn't it?"

So much for the 'fake it' bit. "It is, yes, of course it is. It's just that—"

"You don't look like it's a good thing." Her employer angled her head. "If that's a smile it's turned upside down."

The same green eyes Jenna thrust from her thoughts earlier reappeared above a grin loaded with enough trouble and charm to stir any red-blooded female's hormones up. "If that's a smile, you're doing it wrong; it's upside down. Here, let me fix it for you." Even at that age Chase's whiskey smooth voice had been as full of promise and sin as the rest of him and he never missed an opportunity to tease - or kiss - a smile out of her.

Stop it already. Why couldn't she get that man of her head lately?

"Jenna?"

Jenna's focus snapped back with a start. "Huh? Oh...I'm sorry, what were you saying?"

One penciled on eyebrow shot up and the other scrunched down. "Gracious Jenna, it's not like you to be so distracted. The art show? Is it a good thing or not, dear?"

"The show. Right. Well yes—"

The raised brow joined its lowered twin, creating an all out grimace on Mrs. Goreman's face.

"Guess you know me too well, huh?" Jenna turned to lean against her own car and scraped gravel with the toe of her shoe. "You see, with the gallery shutting down, being able to come up with the entry fee might be a bit of an issue is all."

Mrs. Gorman's face fell. "Oh my. Oh dear." She started to twist the handle of her purse. "I feel terrible about this. I guess I wasn't thinking, but of course you'd be losing income while the repairs were made. Oh Jenna, I wish there was something I could do, but with the HVAC giving us grief I—"

Jenna, wishing she had kept her mouth shut, gently worked her friend's fingers free of the innocent purse strap and gave them a reassuring squeeze. "It's not your fault the HVAC system is on the fritz and who knew I'd suddenly need extra cash at precisely the same time. I sure didn't."

Jenna leaned over and opened the door to Mrs. G.'s car, and with a gentle nudge guided her until she was safely in the driver's seat. "Hey, think maybe that new beau of yours knows someone who'd hire me for a week?"

Mrs. Goreman clapped her hand to her forehead. "Oh! Hold the darn phone, what a ninny. Why didn't I think of this sooner? Never mind Mr. Deagal, I know someone." With amazing agility for someone her age she dove across the seat and yarded the glove box open.

Rooting around with a great deal of grunting, groaning and 'for pity sake-ing' Mrs. Goreman at last righted herself and presented her prize. "Here Jenna, now you give this gal a call. She's the daughter, of the sister, of the lady I sit next to in church and from what Mabel, her mother says, she's always looking for people who have a good eye and a way with a camera. And you take such lovely pictures for your sculpture studies, you'll be in like Flint."

Jenna turned the plain white cardboard square over and read it. 'Models to Go' a Division of 'Theatre to Go'. Marla Gibson, Agent. 405-555-7399.

Photographer for a modeling agency?

Had someone told her a week ago she'd be in the art show the same year the Stampede celebrated its hundredth anniversary and would suddenly become a fashion photographer, she'd have laughed in their face.

But what the heck, what did she have to lose?

Disoriented and sweating, Jenna struggled upright out of her twisted blankets and looked around the moonlit room. Only when she started to recognize the familiar shapes of her loft did let out the breath she'd been holding.

"It was a dream."

Like always she could swear a hint of his warm leather and pine scent lingered in the air and the heat from him holding her in his arms still warmed her skin. "It was just a dream."

Jenna scrubbed her hands down her face and they came away wet with tears. Who was she kidding? That was no dream, it was a nightmare. One she hadn't had for a long time.

It always started with Chase making love to her that first time and ended with him ripped from her arms and vanishing into a black hole where she couldn't follow. Grabbing a tissue from her night stand Jenna wiped the moisture from her face and worked on gaining control over her racing heart.

Next time she decided to call Tina and try to make sense of her life over drinks it would have to be somewhere other than the bar the girl worked at. Cowboys may be the most fun *she* could have with her boots on, but to Jenna it obviously stirred up things better left alone.

Untangling herself from the mangled mess of her bedclothes, Jenna stood on wobbly legs to grab some water and an aspirin but ended up drifting past the kitchen toward her studio on the opposite end of the loft instead.

Cold harsh light from the almost full moon shone on the drop cloth covering the one piece she could never quite bring herself to finish.

Standing in front of it, she pulled the canvas shroud away. It was a stupid thing to do, but she reached out and skimmed her hand over broad shoulders and down the lean line of sculpted muscle to base of the spine.

There'd be a scar there now.

Memories flooded her mind and her hand trembled as the play of light and shadow flowed over the masculine arms encircling the neck of a stallion. The sense of oneness between the two she'd created still captured her imagination every time she looked at it.

Her fingers followed the ends of the man's hair where it fell straight to his shoulder blades then back up to where it joined and merged into one with the horse's mane. She continued over the top of the stallion's pointed ears and down the arc of its neck. The melding of the two into one had turned out even better than she'd hoped.

It would've been called 'Wild Hearts' if she'd ever finished it.

Only part of the man's face could be seen from the side, shadowed as it was by the equine face over his right shoulder but it was clearly recognizable. Chase had been her best friend all through junior high and high school. And for a wonderful but

16

painfully short time after they graduated, he'd been her lover and the man she intended to spend the rest of her life with.

Everything had seemed so perfect. They both loved ranching and the wild open land of southern Alberta they'd grown up in. They both loved art and horses, her more so the art and him the horses, but it hadn't mattered. Between them, it all balanced out.

They were young and loved each other to distraction. They spend numerous days and nights planning for the future, anticipating all the wonderful adventures ahead of them. They'd even set the wedding date. July 19th, the Saturday after that year's Stampede.

A cloud darkened the moon's rays; flattening out the three dimensional effect and illusion of life it had lent the piece, breaking the spell. Dropping her hand Jenna reached down and tossed the tarp back over the sculpture before turning her back on it.

Why was she doing this to herself? What was she thinking? She really should get rid of it.

Just like he'd gotten rid of her.

Chapter 2

"The hell you say!"

Chase paused mid-turn and looked longingly at the light at the end of the tunnel, or in this case the open barn door. Even if he made a mad dash for freedom, there was no hope he'd make it before the verbal storm surging at his back broke over him.

Instead he took a last look through the grain-dust motes filtering the sunny foothills beyond, and sighed. Dropping his chin, he dragged the well-loved black Stetson from his head and braced himself for the onslaught.

"Lord-a-mighty boy, you lost your mind!" The pitch fork Jacob Tuttle had been wielding with the gusto of a man twice his size and half his age hit the dirt floor with a thud. "You've had some dumb-assed notions in your time, but this one's just plain stupid."

A snort, sounding suspiciously like a snicker, and a burst of oat scented air wafted in Chase's face. Moon Dancer, the four year old stallion in the stall to his right, had apparently decided a front row seat for JT's rant was more enticing than his feed bucket.

The horse's obsidian eyes sparkled and he

bobbed his head, sending his silver forelock flapping. Another snort ended in a lip curl no one could mistake for anything but an equine smirk.

"Think this is funny, do you?" Chase leaned closer and pointed with his hat. "Just remember, smart guy, when he finishes chewing me a new one, he'll be putting you through your paces so I wouldn't laugh if I were you." The horse's ears swiveled flat, he gave his mane a quarter shake, and stomped his front hoof. Chase bit the inside of his lip to stop from grinning. Only people who'd never been around them thought horses were dumb.

"You're damn right I'm gonna chew you a new one." JT stomped up in front of the stall, and glanced over his shoulder at the nosey horse. "And you, ya smart ass, mind your own business." Then, turning his attention back on Chase he crossed his arms and squinted.

Chase bit harder. What he wouldn't give for a camera right now. At just over five feet tall, the irate ranch hand now had Dancer's chin practically resting on the crown of his hat. They looked like one of those caricatures you could get at the Stampede.

"Guess once wasn't good enough for you, huh?"

19

Chase's twitching lip flattened. He'd hoped there'd be a way around this but as usual it had been wishful thinking. The man had always believed in cutting right to the heart of the matter. "JT—"

"All them doctors, with all their schooling, didn't know what they were talking about, that it?"

"That's not—"

JT's voice got louder with each interruption and Dancer's head judiciously disappeared behind the stall gate. "Oh. Wait, I get it. By some miracle, Chuckwagon racing is suddenly accident proof." Working himself into a good lather now, he started flapping his arms. "So, guess there's no need to worry about you winding up back in that chair for good this time, is there."

Chase concentrated on keeping his own temperature from rising. He knew he had some lumps coming, and because the man was the father of his heart, he'd take them. But if JT honestly thought Chase *wanted* to head out on the track again, he was being an idiot. "JT damn it, I'm not doing this for kicks; I need the money—"

"And the only way to get it is to go back on your word and risk your fool neck!"

On the heels of JT's bellow a swallow burst from the rafters and shot out the door. The barn

20

filled with a cavernous silence and even the grasshoppers outside stopped chirping.

Chase squeezed his eyes shut trying to block out the ghost of beeping monitors and his mother's rasping struggle to draw enough breath to speak. "Chase...you look at me. Promise me...promise me you...won't...go back. Hear me?"

The memory of her skeletal hand clutching his arm as she voiced her final plea chilled him. "You're the...last Donavan...all that's left. Don't let it take...you too. Don't let it all end...like that. For...nothing. Promise...me."

How could he deny her dying wish? He couldn't.

"For the first time since she passed, I'm glad your Mama isn't here."

Chase felt as hollow as the sound of JT's receding footsteps. "So am I."

Chase sat on the edge of the desk and planted his boot on the window ledge. It had taken all of five minutes for JT to rake him over the proverbial coals then over an hour to settle the horses down in the wake of his tirade. Pure blood lines and

21

someone bellowing at the top of their lungs never mixed well.

They'd managed to avoid each other for the rest of the day but neither man was the type to let things go unsettled for long. Besides, Chase already felt rotten enough about what he had to do. He didn't want JT pissed at him on top of it.

He could see the stubborn old bugger kicking dirt around out in the paddock after putting Dancer back in his stall for the night. He could practically hear the muttered half sentences he was undoubtedly chewing on out there. "Damn fool kid...brains like oatmeal...kick his damn ass...known mules less stubborn...."

Another ten minutes and if JT didn't come in, he'd suck it up, be the bigger man and go out to him. Didn't mean he'd like it, in fact he'd just as soon eat one of the loose fence boards for dinner, but he'd do it anyway.

Chase really hoped JT'd give in first.

He looked away from the source of his current frustration to the clutter-heavy shelves across the room. They hadn't changed since as long as he could remember. Old photos and yellowed sketches, in various stages of completion, depicting everything from horses and ranch life, to mountain scenes and *her* greeted him.

Jenna-Lynn.

A pain in the vicinity of the third rib on his left side gave him a sharp jab.

All of it, especially the girl, belonged in the past. One where he still believed he had choices in life. But Lord how he wished things had turned out different.

Not wanting to pick at that old wound his gaze shifted to the ribbons, trophies and snapshot parade of mismatched frames showing his family before things had gone to hell.

The largest showed a tall broad-shouldered man with blond hair and an infectious smile. His father, Ian Patrick Donavan, had been a stubborn hard drinking rancher and man's man, who'd worshipped his wife and loved his sons. But not enough to keep him off the circuit that finally killed him.

In the picture he stood in front of an aluminum clad travel trailer with his left arm loosely draped around a laughing young woman, as dark as he was fair. Lita Little-Bird Donavan, their mother, so young, carefree and beautiful staring back at Chase from out of the past. She had been the glue that held them all together and the only thing that kept them even close to tamed.

His father's other hand was poking at a gangly teenager to his right. The teen, light in coloring like the man, had his arms crossed in front of his chest and the look on his face seemed less about sucking on a lemon as having one up his skinny butt. Ryan, his older brother was always running to follow in the old man's footsteps. He'd made it to the ripe old age of twenty-three before he followed him all the way to his own early grave.

The last member of the group, a younger boy with wild dark hair, knobby elbows, and pants several inches too short, was tugging his mouth wide and sticking his tongue out while crossing his eyes at the camera.

A small smile flirted with Chase's lips and for a moment he was that innocent boy again. At the age where all things 'bodily function' was hilarious, he'd been a royal pain that whole summer. Arm pit farts, practical jokes and burp fests had been the order of the day. Had life ever been that simple?

His fledgling grin faded before it had a chance to fully develop. It was also the first year he'd been considered old enough to ride with his dad and brother in the real events. He'd felt so grown up, and proud to officially be one of the Donavan boys.

If he'd known what was to come of it, he'd have kept his ass out of the saddle and stuck with his charcoal pencils.

"Chase? You back there boy?"

JT's bark came from the old part of the barn constructed when the Flying D Ranch was nothing but a farmstead. Over a hundred years later, with the Donavan boys racking up the trophies and prize money, it's new section, complete with an office and separate staging area beyond big enough for two full wagon teams, had been added. Too bad *they* hadn't known then what *he* knew now. They might not have done it.

Chase stole one last glance at the past, before he stepped back behind the desk, sucked in a steadying breath, and for the first time in his life felt the weight of sitting down in his father's chair. "Yah."

JT's boots clunked across the plank floors and Chase heard him long before his face was around the corner. "Okay, here's the way I see it. You're going about this all wrong boy. See, ya gotta examine all sides of a problem before choosing your trail. You know, take it apart one bit at a time."

He didn't slow down or look up as he entered the room but he did whip his hat off his head and started spinning it in his hands, about as close to making a concession as JT was likely to come. "What about Ian's insurance money?"

"Gone, I'm afraid. Apparently Mom had been using it to keep things afloat a lot longer than she let on."

"Oh. What about the bank then, have you tried asking for an extension?"

"After she died I called them. We were already three months behind then, and not for the first time. Best the bank manager could offer was to hold off till the end of July before starting formal foreclosure proceedings.

"And that was only after I said I'd been offered a spot with a top wagon heading into the Stampede. Which, by the way, even if Jared's canvas did take top money, my outrider's share would still only buy us another month or two at most."

"Well, ain't that all fine and dandy. Then what?" To his credit, it didn't take long for the other shoe to drop and JT's whiskers to start bristling.

"Oh no. Hold on a damn minute." He knocked the pile of newspapers and magazine's off the only other chair in the room, anchored himself to the seat and scooted the whole issue forward till he was staring Chase directly in the eye across the desk.

"We're not talking about just the Rangeland Derby here are we? That'd be one thing. But, oh no, you aim to hit the full circuit again don't you? That's what you're saying to me isn't it?"

In light of the setting sun behind him, for the first time, Chase noticed the signs of age and worry etched into his friend's face. It wasn't a comforting sight and his comeback held more bite than intended.

"Look JT, if you can come up with some other way around this, I'm all ears." Ticking off a count on his fingers Chase laid things out. "There's no money to subdivide the main parcel, Mom's small section at Coyote Pass has sentimental value to her people and even if I was willing to sell it, I couldn't without her father's co-signature. And since he disowned her for marrying Dad and hasn't wanted anything to do with us since, we both know that's not going to happen—"

"Hmph. Miserable old coot." JT turned his head as though he was about to spit then thought better of it and swallowed instead. "Sorry, throat's dry."

Chase leaned over, opened the bottom drawer of the desk and pulled out a bottle of bourbon. Pouring two shots he handed one over to JT who

27

knocked it back in one go.

"There's only two other options I can see, one is to accept the offer from Gord Hogan who wants me to stud Dancer out to him."

JT looked like he had something sour in his mouth and he skidded further forward in his chair. "The hell you say! That's the second dumbest thing I ever heard come outta your mouth today. That stallion's a Thoroughbred, by God; a born racer!" He waved his hat as though swatting a fly out of the air. "Not one of them prissy ass jumpers, so you tell Mr. Fancy Pants Hogan there he can forget it."

Chase couldn't help but grin at all the clucking and flapping going on. The old cuss was constantly saying he had no use for 'that mangy stallion's ornery hide' and Dancer seemed to go out of his way to be as contrary back. Like siblings, they could poke at each other, but heaven help anyone else who tried it.

"Simmer down and don't get your shirt in a knot old timer. If we can pull this thing out, we'll need his bloodline to rebuild our breeding program, so you can relax." Watching the wind come out of JT's sail's would've been comical if the topic weren't so serious.

"Hmph. That's something I guess." JT

narrowed his eyes. "And you watch your mouth boy. I'm not such an old timer I can't still whup your scrawny ass." After reestablishing the pecking order, JT accepted another shot from Chase then chuckled. "I know. You could always give that little gal that wanted to sell your purdy face a call. She said you could make a fortune off that mug of yours."

Chase choked on his own drink and sputtered as he wiped his chin on his sleeve. "Yeah right, like I'd ever be able to live that down."

"Okay, okay. I was just kiddin' with ya. So what's left then, the cattle?"

"You know the herd's already been thinned down so far that if I sell any more we won't be able to sustain it. Then what do we do long term? No herd. No ranch."

JT's face fell and his chest seemed to cave in on itself. "Huh, I see your point."

God love him, what JT lacked in youth he made up for in stubborn but if Chase didn't keep a close eye on him, the old cuss wouldn't stop till he dropped. That was something he simply couldn't let happen.

Chase switched on the lamp against the looming shadows and tossed a piece of paper down so the words faced JT. "The absolute last resort is to sell out completely. Rocky Meadows Riding Stables to the north is interested, but only in the whole operation. They want to expand and open a full service guest ranch."

JT's Adam's apple visibly bobbed in slow motion and his lips thinned till they turned as white as the rest of his complexion. His engine sputtering, he made three false starts before the words finally made it out whole. "You...you can't...you wouldn't...."

Wait for it. Three, two, one—

JT shot straight out of his chair as though he'd sat on his pitch fork. "I should bloody well hope that's the last resort Chase. Damn it, boy. Your daddy, his daddy and his before him didn't work their asses off to have their legacy turned into some city slicker style tourist trap...dude ranch!"

Grabbing his opening, Chase leaned on his elbows and modulated his voice. "So we agree then. My riding with Jared's rig is the only real option we have right now."

Chase watched the gears turn as the reality of their circumstances sunk in until JT's hands fell to his sides. "Guess that's that then."

He came around the desk and clapped his hand

on JT's shoulder hoping the doubt he felt inside didn't come out in his voice. "Let's take it one step at a time. We'll concentrate on getting through the Stampede, buy ourselves some time and go from there. We're not beat yet and who knows, maybe some other solution will present itself in the mean time." *Please let something else present itself.*

JT looked him in the eye and swallowed hard. "Okay boy, we'll do it your way. I don't like it, but can't say I see any other way clear neither." Shrugging out from under Chase's hand, JT put his hat back on his head and melted silently into the deep shadows of the barn.

Bone weary after his nineteen hour day, Chase sank back down in his chair. It was a done deal now. For better or worse, he was rejoining the Wild Bunch, outriders for the famous chuckwagon racers. Guys crazy enough to launch themselves onto the backs of ex-race horses, haul out after wagons pulled by more high strung thoroughbreds, all tearing at breakneck speed around an oval track and calling it fun.

Flashbacks of the tragedies his family had suffered surfaced; living nightmares filled with screaming horses, wailing sirens and searing pain in his back. Terror brought on by the numbing cold where he lost the feeling in his right leg that night, spinning wheels silhouetted against the sky and the horrified silence of a crowded grandstand.

He knew first hand why it was called 'The Half Mile of Hell'. He'd been on the sidelines watching when the first accident took his dad. Then smack dab in the middle of the second, which killed his brother and left Chase in a wheel chair facing an agonizing year of physiotherapy before he could walk again. His mother wasn't the only one who didn't want him to race again. The thought of it woke him up at night in a cold sweat.

Chase held his glass up and looked through the remaining amber liquid to the pictures on the shelf beyond. "If you could find me another way, Mom, I'd gladly take it."

Knocking back the shot he went to set the empty glass on the desk and accidentally knocked the lid off the bottle onto the floor.

His father had drilled into their heads that if you tossed a lid away you'd best be prepared to kill off the bottle because no man wasted good whiskey by letting it evaporate out. His dad had lived by that sentiment.

Chase reached down and swept his hand under the chair. "Damn." Now was not the time to risk the wrath of the whiskey gods. He rummaged under the desk where he thought the lid escaped and finally felt something brush the edge of his hand. Closing his fingers around it he sat back up to discover it wasn't the only thing he'd retrieved.

A crumpled business card had come along for the ride. After putting the lid back on the bourbon and putting it away. Chase smoothed out the little piece of white cardboard and held it closer to the light.

'Models to Go' a Division of 'Theatre to Go'. Marla Gibson, Talent Scout. 405-555-7399.

Are you kidding me? Chase started to laugh, then thought; what the hell, what did he have to lose? Nothing.

Unless of course anyone found out about it.

Chapter 3

Confirming the address on the card, Jenna pulled up in front of an older sandstone and brick building located in a light industrial area and parked her little hatchback. Inside, the lobby sported a trendy mix of 'worn-out warehouse' and modern Italian design that appealed to her artist's eye.

She looked past a massive granite block with a listing of the floor and suite numbers of the businesses situated within and spotted an old fashioned elevator platform complete with a grillwork cage door. One obviously designed for lifting freight not people.

It could hold Marty the moose and half his family for goodness sake and Jenna stumbled as the thing lurched into motion.

After a harrowing ride of shudders and clunks, she stepped off into a hallway capped by a ceiling so high the light from the sconces running the length of the walls could barley reach it. What was this place originally used for anyway, herding elephants?

The muffled rhythmic thump of music coming from the far end caught her attention, hinting at which of the massive metal doors held a fashion studio behind it. A minor tremor scuttled up Jenna's spine and she considered getting back on the elevator.

The entire morning she'd been second guessing herself. Was this a dumb idea? Was she wasting valuable time? After all, what did she know about fashion photography? Sure she'd done some photo work in art school and since then, plenty of study shots for her own use, but that was a totally different thing.

Oh Jenna quit procrastinating. It won't hurt to at least go talk to the woman.

Squaring her shoulders, she marched to the end of the hall and read 'Models to Go' on the ten by ten steel door which seemed to slide sideways of its own accord. The maelstrom of camera flashes, pounding music and blur of motion within shocked her after the cavernous stillness everywhere else in the building.

Barely inside the door Jenna was so startled by the sea of modern Amazons and Greek gods in various stages of undress before her, she froze and only vaguely registered someone brushing past her shoulder and the door closing behind her.

Talk about Hollywood north. Jenna hadn't felt this inadequate since they forced spandex running shorts on her high school gym class.

"Hello, can I help you?"

A woman wearing a wireless headset popped up in front of her. She was as gorgeous as the others but so short, Jenna wondered how she didn't get lost among the giants around her.

Her gamine face lit with a pleasant and knowing smile. "First time at a modeling studio huh?"

Jenna took an instant liking to her and smiled back. "That obvious?"

The woman winked and stuck out her hand "Don't worry. Everyone gets a bit overwhelmed when they first behold the genetically over-gifted brigade. My name is Tamra Eaton, how can I help you?"

Jenna returned the gesture then pulled the card out of her purse. "I'm Jenna Cordell, I'm here to see Margo Gibson—"

"Oh Ms. Cordell, she's been expecting you, please come right this way." Tamra spun on her heel, waving her hand ahead of her to clear a path. Jenna had no choice but to follow quickly or be cut off from her guide.

~*~*~

Entering the building, Chase glanced back over his shoulder and hoped he wouldn't find a ticket on the windshield of his truck when he returned. There was no room for him to park in front and the only other option was a loading zone on the other side of the street.

Once his eyes adjusted to the inside of the windowless lobby, he frowned at the furniture beside him. What was it about city people putting ridiculously expensive leather couches in the middle of dilapidated warehouses? The top of his boot was higher than the seats on the dumb things. How the hell was a man supposed to sit down on that without wrapping his knees around his ears?

And what was the sense in plunking a great big rock in front of the elevators? Shaking his head, Chase boarded and pushed the button for the top floor. As the gate clanged shut and he started his ascent, he took his hat off and wiped his brow with the back of his hand. Had this really seemed like a good idea last night?

The previous evening's bourbon was playing havoc with his skull, and he was beginning to wonder if JT was right about him needing his head read.

The elevator shuddered to a stop and Chase

found 'Models to Go' at the far end of the hallway. He pulled the sliding door open and stopped dead in his tracks, no longer doubting it. What the hell was he doing here? There were half naked women everywhere!

Before he could bring himself to look away, one of them, a leggy blond almost as tall as he was, yanked her skimpy shirt off and tossed it to a little bald guy running along behind her. Two of the perkiest breasts Chase had ever seen now stood at attention directly in front of him.

"Hurry up Mel, I only have one minute to change, and where the hell's Justine with my make-up?"

He'd had his fair share of experience with the opposite sex, but damn; even a man with far more than him would be left with his jaw nailed to his chest at that sight.

As the woman charged past him, the torpedoes leading the way were hardly moving. Chase's face heated and he ducked behind the brim of his hat. Crap he'd been staring like a teenager ogling his first Playboy centerfold.

"You! Don't move."

Chase looked up to find a woman with a microphone curled in front of her face bearing down on him. A quick glance behind him confirmed there was nobody else there, so he turned back toward the tiny figure, now pointing a computer tablet at him and swallowed. Had she noticed his lack of manners? He hoped not. The fact she was short didn't do a thing to lessen her intensity. He'd faced wild bulls that made him less nervous.

"Ma'am?"

Without slowing her forward momentum, she reached for his arm. "Yes, you; and if you're who I think you are—"

Upon contact with his wrist she stopped and raised her eyebrows, it looked way too thick in her grip. Even with nails half the length of her fingers, she could barely wrap her hand around it. Giving him a head to toe scan, she settled for a tugging on his shirt sleeve instead. "Whew, even if you aren't him, I'll pay her the five bucks anyway."

His head spinning, Chase didn't protest as she herded him into a nearby office. "Excuse me, him who?" With a gentle shove 'elf-girl' proved that his knees really did come up to his ears when he sat on one of these Italian monstrosities.

He landed awkwardly, and had to cradle his good hat so he didn't accidentally crush it as he tipped sideways. The woman was already streaking

39

out the door. "Excuse me, but—"

"Now you sit tight sugar, I'll be right back." The rest of her words drifted back from the reception area beyond his field of vision. "Mel. Don't let this guy leave."

Don't let this guy leave? Chase bristled. He'd leave if he ruddy well wanted to. He'd had enough. This had been a stupid idea in the first place and time for this cowboy to hit the road.

He shoved hard only to end up listing to the side again. Gritting his teeth, he crammed his hat back on his head and tried again. This time, the smooth soles of his boots slipped out from under him and sent his heels skidding on the polished marble floor.

Cursing, he grabbed tight to the edge of the seat and kicked his long legs out thinking enough momentum would propel him to a standing position.

Instead his jeans slid on the polished leather sending him slumping further down into the cushions and pushing his hat forward over his face.

Flopping around like a new born colt, Chase clamped his jaw shut holding in a tantrum any two year old would be proud of and struggled to scoot his boots back toward him while trying to right his hat with a shake of his head.

All he got for his efforts was a headache and his one leg bent like a pretzel.

Knocking his hat off so he could see again, Chase sighed and took stock of his situation. Damn it. He was getting out of here and that was that.

Just as soon as he figured out how to hog tie a bloody couch.

Marla Gibson's perfectly manicured fingers flipped through Jenna's portfolio at a measured pace. The only real indication she liked what she saw was an occasional nod of her head and tug on her bejeweled ear lobe. At least Jenna hoped that was what it meant.

"I can certainly appreciate your artistic eye, Ms. Cordell. You have a great understanding of composition and light as well as a natural touch for capturing both the subject and a sense of emotion." Removing her reading glasses, Marla squinted at Jenna and sat back in her chair.

Jenna's heart sank. This wouldn't be the first time someone claimed to love her work as they wished her the best of luck and showed her the door.

41

Several suspended seconds passed before Marla shifted forward and toyed with the arms on her glasses. "And I appreciate your honesty about only being interested in a temporary assignment. My main concern is that I may not be able to offer you enough work in the next week to make it worth your while."

Like that mattered. On her way here Jenna had tried to think of other things she might want to do to make extra money, only to concede, any work was better than no work. But before she could plead her case, Tamra burst in. "Marla! Oh my god girl, you are so not going to believe who I think just walked in here."

Marla's head snapped up. "Pardon me? Couldn't this have waited a few minutes? I'm with someone here."

Unabashed Tamra turned to Jenna. "Ms. Cordell, please forgive the intrusion, but I'm afraid this matter simply couldn't wait." She shot a smug look at Marla. "And for the record, Boss, if I'm right you *will* thank me for this."

An alarming mottled pattern crept across Marla's cheeks. "Tamra, what it is you're on about, and it better be good."

The younger woman crossed her arms over her

chest and smirked. "Do the words 'six foot four, tanned, dark haired, bulging hunk of muscle in a black hat and cowboy boots' mean anything to you?"

"Oh for pity's sake girl, would you spit it out. What are you talking about?"

A giggle escaped Tamra's lips. "Okay, because of the sizzling hot authentic cowboy type Mel has corralled out there I'm fairly certain I've lost our bet and owe you five bucks. You know, the one where I said the guy you gave your card to at that rodeo would never darken our door and you said he would."

Marla stood slowly and came around the side of her desk. "Do you mean who I think you do?"

Tamra winked, hooked her thumbs in the front pockets of her jeans and started rocking back and forth at the hips. "You're darn tootin' I do."

Marla went eerily still and a calculating look flitted across her face. "Ms. Cordell, I'm hoping you won't mind our taking a break." With a well practiced flick, she held out a card sandwiched between her fingers. "However, I'll certainly understand if you've prior commitments and have to go. But if you do, please call me tomorrow. I have a funny feeling we may be able to work something out after all."

Jenna accepted the card and looked at her watch. Her only other commitment was with the want ads, but she didn't want to appear completely desperate either. "If you don't think it'll be too long, I suppose I could stay a bit longer."

"Fabulous!" Marla clapped her hands once and spun on her assistant as she charged through the door. "Tamra where—"

"Front office." Tamra leaned out the door and called down the hall after Marla. "And yes, I'll show Ms. Cordell to the lounge, but not until I see if I'm right."

Feeling awkward, Jenna decided maybe some cold water on her heated face would help her regain her bearings before deciding what her next step should be. "You go ahead. I'd like to freshen up a bit anyway so if you could point me the direction of a ladies room I'll meet you back out in the reception area in a few minutes if that works?"

"Perfect." Tamra pointed randomly down the opposite hall as she shot out after Marla. "Rest rooms are to the right around the corner."

~*~*~

Chase thought the little one with the microphone was scary; Marla Gibson made her look positively docile.

In a blur he'd gone from rolling to his belly - the only way he'd finally been able to extract himself from hell-couch - to standing here shaking hands with his new boss, err, agent, all in a matter of minutes.

In less time than it took him to jump on Moon Dancer's back, she'd explained about the whole modeling thing. Part of him was still uncomfortable with the idea, while another part wondered why he hadn't done something like this before.

"I'm so glad you reconsidered my offer Mr. Donavan. All you need to do is sign here and you'll be part of the 'Models to Go' family." With a polished smile, Marla released his hand and seemed to produce a pen out of the air.

"Please, Chase will do." He accepted the brandished implement as she spun the contract toward him and pointed at the signature line. His hand hovered over the paper and a hint of caution unfurled in his gut. "Now, forgive me if I'm repeating what you already told me, but I want to be sure I have it all straight."

"Hmm?" Her smile never faltered as she inched

the contract closer to him.

"I'm agreeing to model for you, but not in person, only in photographs, which you can use for any campaign you see fit." A picture of himself on the cover of some boy toy magazine popped into his mind and a burst of heat crept up the back of his neck. It was all he could do not to reach up and rub it. "But at no time will they be used for anything porn...uh, let's say no place I couldn't show my Grandma."

Great, now his face had joined in the action. Why was it a guy could say all kinds of vulgar things around other guys, but with a woman he got all tongue tied? He'd damn near put 'Grandma' and 'pornography' in the same sentence.

He tipped his head down further. Maybe she hadn't noticed him blushing. "And we also agree that at no time will my face be seen right? Just the rest of me showing off clothes or holding onto some product or something. Right?"

Did her smile falter? He blinked and the impression was gone.

"Absolutely Chase." As though sensing his hesitance, she stopped short of pushing the paper again and stepped back. "You can certainly have someone look over the contract if you'd like before signing it, of course." Marla circled the desk and rested her hand on his shoulder. "But, I can assure you we're on the same page. We both agree I have complete say over what photographers, makeup people and campaigns etc - who of course are all bound to my end of the agreement - and you agree to work with all of us for our mutual financial gain; also within the confines of our agreement. Yes?"

She had thrown some impressive numbers at him over the last several minutes and he'd already figured out how fast the ranch could be back on its feet if he did this. Add in the anonymity she promised and there was really no reason not to go ahead with it. Right?

Never mind right; he needed the money and that was that.

Chase adjusted the contract on an angle and quickly signed his name to it before his better judgment followed his original impulse and sent him hightailing out the door.

The pen was out of his hand practically before he'd finished lifting it from the document. "Wonderful. I'll have legal get you a copy before you leave." She grabbed his suddenly empty hand and gave it a quick squeeze. "You won't regret it Chase."

Pressing a button on the phone brought Tamra and her energy buzz through the door. "So, Boss, do we have a new MG member, or what?"

"We do, and I want to get him set up immediately for the 'Wild' campaign. Have Mel schedule wardrobe with Georgie first thing tomorrow and I want Katrina to do his grooming and makeup."

Tamra consulted her tablet. "Okay, I'll put Justine on her morning clients then. Who's shooting?"

"You arrange the rest and let me worry about the photographer."

Tamra's eyebrow lifted. "Okay, whatever you say, you're the boss."

It was like they'd forgotten he was in the room. Marla snatched up the contract and waved it in the air. "Oh, and Mr. Donavan will need a copy of this before he leaves today."

Tamra took it from her and poked his shoulder as she slid past on her way out of the office. "And, you cowboy, owe me a latte. You cost me five bucks."

As soon as she'd left, Marla moved in and patted his bewildered face; the motherly gesture at odds with the gleam in her eye. "You and I are

48

going to make a lot of money together, handsome. And don't worry, you can trust me."

A thread of unease rippled under his skin as he reached for his hat. Man he sure hoped so because he'd never be able to show his face again if anyone ever found about this. He'd be so embarrassed, JT might as well geld him and stick him out to pasture.

Chapter 4

Jenna checked her watch again; another fifteen minutes had gone by. It had been over an hour since she'd found the ladies' room then returned to the waiting area and still no sign of either Tamra or Marla.

If she hung around any longer she really would look as desperate as she felt. Resigned, Jenna reached down for her purse deciding she'd give Marla a call in the morning.

She headed for the door and out of nowhere a pair of breasts slammed into Jenna's forehead knocking her backwards, sending her arms flailing in a vain effort to stay upright and her purse flying through the air.

"Watch it!" The Breast-beast snarled and kept going without as much as a backward glance.

Jenna braced herself for the impact, but before she hit the ground, a pair of tree-trunk arms clamped around her midsection from behind. Instead of landing on cold marble, she was pulled up tight against another hard surface. This one a brick wall of heated muscle.

"Whoa darlin', easy there."

The puff from his words tickled her neck and

the deep timbre of his voice vibrated straight through Jenna's bones. The scent of tanned leather and a hint of fresh air wrapped around her, she wanted to drag it deep into her lungs and hold it there till her head spun.

Her heartbeat sped up at the feel of the thick cords of his forearms moving under her hands and fired her adrenaline into overdrive faster than the initial threat of falling on her butt had.

Standing her up, the man reached down to retrieve her purse and its scattered contents before she had a chance to turn around and see his face. The arms were good, but if the face was half as good as the set of perfect male buns aimed at her, female-kind was in serious trouble.

No butt had a right to fill out a pair of jeans like that without a warning label.

Jenna you ninny, you're standing here drooling while the poor man is picking up your stuff.

Cheeks blazing at her lapse, Jenna dove in. "Oh, wait, you don't need to do that. I can get it from here." On her hands and knees she ran her hand under the low sofa to make sure nothing had rolled out of sight.

"It's no bother, I'm just glad you weren't hurt. This marble floor isn't very forgiving. Trust me, I

51

know." A flicker of familiarity rippled up her spine at his soft chuckle. He leaned over her back and dangled her purse in front of her. "Here you go."

"Ahhh!" Jenna jumped and struck her head on something hard.

"Ouch!"

His chin? Those steel bands came around her for the second time and all too soon, he stood up bringing her to her feet with him.

Before Jenna could turn and make sure she hadn't broken the nose of her rescuer, Marla was in front of her. "You're still here Ms. Cordell, wonderful. And I see you two have met, fabulous."

The wall of flesh at her back froze. "Ms. Cordell?"

Jenna's heart stopped with a painful thud. She *did* know that voice. But, no, it couldn't be. Could it? The man who held her slowly turned her toward him and if he hadn't still been holding her she would've ended up on her butt after all.

"Jenna-Lynn?"

Jenna was speechless. The face of her knight in shining armor was that of the handsome-as-sin cowboy she'd worked so hard to drive from her mind.

Face to face with the flesh and blood version of

her nightly dreams Jenna realized she'd been kidding herself. And being in this particular cowboy's arms was the most dangerous place on earth because it was a place she'd never stopped longing to be.

"Jen? Is it really you?"

Phantoms of all the naïve plans and wishes they'd shared were reflected in the forest green depths of his eyes and the wonder on his beautiful face broke her heart all over again. It was almost like the tragedy that had torn them apart had never happened.

But something was off. Confusion rose up to wash away her illusion but brought no clarity. Then it hit her. He was *standing* in front of her. But that was impossible...or a miracle.

Or he'd lied to her.

A thousand memories and feelings collided through Chase at once. Jenna smiling, Jenna laughing, Jenna singing, Jenna crying....

Jenna leaving.

Chase didn't know if he should grab her tighter, or choke her.

53

Gone were the long braids and slightly pudgy cheeks she'd had as a girl and she'd lost all the coltish awkwardness.

Instead her hair was cut short with little wisps of lighter blond curling around her high cheekbones and the subtle hollows beneath made her lush lips more tempting than they'd been before. Her eyes were a deeper blue somehow and bigger than he'd remembered. Eyes currently stretched wide under raised eyebrows in a face gone alarmingly white.

"It can't be."

A small part, deep inside, was gratified her reaction to him being on his feet and not in a damn wheelchair was a shock. At least she wouldn't pity him now; which was something.

It was you who kicked her out, remember?

Yes, but did she have to go so easily?

Jenna squirmed in his grasp and pulled away hugging her arms around herself in the process. "Chase, I can't believe it. It really is you. But how—"

"Correction, apparently you two haven't just met." He'd forgotten Marla was even standing there. "That's even better, you can dispense with the 'get acquainted' stage and get to the working together part."

Jenna's head swiveled at the same speed his did and her voice parroted the words leaving his mouth. "Work together? What do you mean, work together?"

Marla pursed her lips and poked his shoulder with her talon. "You, model." Then she turned that same spike on Jenna. "You, photographer. Simple." She tipped her chin at the reception desk. "Ms. Cordell, there's a file on the counter that explains the *'Wild'* men's cologne campaign and contest photo expectations. Please pick it up on your way out and review it before we meet again at nine A.M. sharp.

"Mr. Donavan...I mean Chase."

Something crept up Chase's neck and he could've sworn a predatory shadow crossed Marla's face.

"You'll need to be in at six for wardrobe and makeup. Tamra will meet you and get you all set up in the morning." With that, a 'tah-tah' and 'have fun' she was gone, leaving him and Jenna in her wake.

Tamra popped up in front before Chase could strike out after Marla and set her straight on a few things. "Whoa there cowboy, I wouldn't bother if I were you. Once she's made up her mind there's no changing it. So whatever personal stuff you two have, I suggest you stow it. You're going to be stuck at the hips for the next few days so you might as well get used to it."

A picture of how he and Jenna might be 'stuck at the hips' flashed through Chase's brain cranking up his frustration level and setting off a low rumble in his throat. A hard-on was the last thing he needed right now.

"I'm no happier about this than you are Chase, but surely, under the circumstances, we can be adults about it. I'm willing if you are. What do you say?"

Jenna's soft voice overrode the no hard-on directive and stroked the area of his brain still rifling through thoughts of their hips and other parts getting together.

Damn it, he should've gotten the hell out of Dodge when he'd had the chance.

Chase had shoved himself as far into the opposite corner of the elevator as possible, Jenna wanted to kick him. If he wanted to keep his distance so bad, why did he keep peeking at her from under the brim of his hat like that?

Jerk.

He'd finally agreed to their working together; only because his contract decreed Marla got to pick who he worked with, but did he have to make it sound like she was dragging him to the electric chair?

Honestly, you'd think she'd tossed him out of her life, not the other way around. Jenna slammed the door on a picture of him lying broken in that hospital bed. Sympathy was over-rated, indignant temper was much better. She should be the one pouting, not him.

At the thought of Chase, the tough guy cowboy, pouting like a little kid a giggle threatened to bubble up her throat. She might have even given into the urge if she weren't worried she'd start crying or pulling her hair out instead.

Of all people, Chase Donavan? Really?

She could already feel the battering her heart would take if she didn't get a grip quick. She desperately needed a reality check. Her Chase, the one she thought she knew, was gone and she'd simply have to come to terms with that. This one might be a bigger, better, more mature version of the one she'd fallen in love with, but four years was

57

a long time and there was no going back. She'd do well to remember that.

Keep telling yourself that and eventually you might believe it.

"Jenna?"

She glanced up and felt her spine stiffen. Oh crap, he was not doing the puppy-dog eye thing was he? He was really playing dirty now. Jenna resisted the urge to swat his hat from his head.

"I'm sorry I was an ass back there. I didn't mean to hurt your feelings; it's not that I'm against working together. That isn't what I meant." He looked down at the floor and shrugged his broad shoulders. "I guess my brain kicked out of gear when I saw you but my mouth didn't get the message and sort of ran off on its own."

Jenna clenched her jaw to keep it from dropping. He was apologizing! She kept her eyes glued on the numbers showing their floor by floor decent and reminded herself not to bite through her tongue. How was she supposed to keep her emotions in check when he was being all nice? He so wasn't fighting fair.

Double jerk.

"Jen did you hear me?" He wrinkled his face and tipped his head from side to side like he used to when they were kids. "Mouth in gear, brain in neutral?"

Oh sure, now he wanted to be funny too. Well she wasn't putting up with that. The nerve. "At least it's nice to know some things never change."

Chase winced. "Ouch."

Out the corner of her eye she saw his hand clutch his chest and his body slump against the wall as the elevator came to a stop on the ground floor. That stupid giggle inside her threatened again as the door opened so she stepped out as quickly as she could, hoping he hadn't noticed.

He caught up to her on the other side of the granite monolith and lifted his hand to grab hers, only to pull back sticking both his in his pockets instead. "Okay, I deserved that." He cocked his head to one side and held it there this time, perfecting the contrite little boy image. "Truce?"

Oh man, he was really hitting below the belt line. And worse, his dirty underhanded trick was working. How was she supposed to resist...well...*that*?

Her imagination ran away with thoughts of *that* and Jenna's mind didn't catch up to her eyes until somewhere in the vicinity of the fourth button of his shirt, where it was busy overlaying a picture of her fingers undoing it.

Her guilty gaze flew to his face and his lips twitched. Busted. The tips of her ears ignited and she wanted to scream.

Of all the arrogant...he knew darn well she could never hold a good mad-on when he flashed those cursed dimples. He was taking unfair advantage.

But she was not about to let him away with it. No siree. No way was she going to smile back. He could forget that.

Jenna choked off the urge to stamp her foot and lifted her chin. "Fine. Since we're working together over the next few days I suppose a temporary truce is in order."

His dimples blew into a full-on impish grin and her own mutinous lips turned her into a liar, breaking the tension in the air.

For the first time since before his accident the warmth she remembered filled his eyes and a thread of it reached out to wrap around her starved heart. Slipping close to their old camaraderie felt so good.

Too good. Not the same man, remember?

Thank goodness he wasn't, otherwise she could easily fall right back in love with him.

Jenna reached for the door but wasn't fast

enough, Chase was there first, his chest a whisper away from brushing up against her back as he opened it for her. "Let me get that." His outdoor scent invaded her head and a tendril of heat unfurled along her spine before curling into a quivering ball low in her belly. What more proof did she need?

The man was a menace.

"Your mother always did let you away with murder when you pulled the gentleman act. Maybe I'll have to have a word with her about it for the sake of unsuspecting woman everywhere.

Chase suddenly seemed a million miles away and his smile was gone. His expression was closed off and guarded as though he'd disappeared behind some kind of wall. What was up with that? "Chase? You okay?"

His voice was void of emotion and tinged with ice as he let the door close behind them and moved past her. "That might be difficult, her being dead and all."

Chapter 5

Chase fought with his conscience all night over being so harsh with Jenna. She'd grown up knowing his mom too and his rudeness had been uncalled for.

Today wasn't working out that well either. As far as he was concerned whoever said things looked better in the morning had never spent one in a beauty salon.

"Oh come on cowboy, it wasn't that bad." Tamra swatted his - now bald - chest with her ever-present computerized clip board. "You, who wrestle bulls the weight of my car for fun, are trying to tell me you can't take a little tweezing." Her eyebrows bounced up and down as she pointed to his oversensitive pects. "Ha! Get it? Tweezing?"

Chase rubbed the tender pink area of his solar plexus and glared at her. "Oh you're a funny one you are. For the record, Tinkerbelle, the bulls weigh more than your car, I wrangle them I don't wrestle them, and they don't pour hot wax all over me then yank my hair out by the roots while I do it."

Leaving yesterday, he'd been convinced this place couldn't get any crazier, now he'd been shampooed, shaved, primped and plucked for god's sake. He couldn't have been more wrong.

She giggled and swatted his backside as she slipped past him. "Whatever Sundance. Suck it up and follow me."

"Sundance?" She was already out the door and Chase had to concentrate on keeping her bobbing ponytail in sight. For a short thing she sure could move.

"If we're going down nickname road, then I'm pegging you Sundance. Deal with it."

He dodged around people coming and going in all directions and he had to yell over the pounding music escaping from the various studio areas. "What, you don't like to be compared to a pretty little thing with wings?"

She shouted back. "What, you don't like to be compared to a romantic western hero?"

Chase snorted. "Romantic? Guy ate a face full of lead in the end if I remember right."

"Uh huh, and the sexy little fairy fell for a guy who refused to grow up and got her butt chucked in a cage for her trouble."

Tamra paused outside the wardrobe room and a strange look crossed her face.

"Been there. Got the striped shirt, yadda, yadda." With a tiny shake of her head, her eyes cleared and the moment passed. "On the other hand,

63

a chick that can fly and has a nasty temper, I can get down with that." A cocky lift of her lip dispelled the last trace of sadness. "And since the gnarly little fairy wouldn't think twice about shooting some smart-ass cowboy like you, I'd get used to Sundance if I were you."

A deep sultry voice ended their banter. "Oh my, Tam-tam you darling girl, what have you brought me today?"

One look at the voice's owner barreling down on him and Chase's opinion on the day got worse. The person was close in height to, but outweighed Chase by several pounds, none of which appeared to be fat.

Tamra stepped back. "Morning Georgie, this is Chase. Told you you'd be glad you were called in to work early today."

Georgie wore thigh-high electric blue suede boots over black stretchy pants and a sleeveless white shirt that laced up the sides. Bright yellow glasses dwarfed the face and several inches of purple-tipped blond hair stuck up in all directions. Except for the purple, it looked like a canary nesting in tumbleweed.

Before Chase could decide if he was looking at a he or a she, Georgie let out a squeak, grabbed him by the shoulders and delivered a Hollywood style 'air-kiss' to each side of his face. "You were right girlfriend. He is pretty."

Pretty? "Wait a minute—"

"And have I got the perfect outfits lined up for him. Everything from the fantastical to the authentic. Gotta give the client lots of looks to choose from, right? Oowheee!" Georgie's large hand wrapped around Chase's arm and tugged him forward into the room. "Now you just come with Georgie."

Before he could get his tongue untied, Chase was swung off his feet and planted on a pedestal in the center of the room facing a three-way mirror. "Now you stay right there handsome." Turning on one high heel, Georgie rubbed his-her hands together then grabbed a cowboy hat with a chin cord, several bandanas and a pair of bright red cowboy boots off the shelf.

Chase gulped. Was he-she kidding?

"These are going to be perfect, and wait till you see the leather vest. Soft as butter and covered in fringes. Oowheee, Darlin'! And matching chaps are to die for, I'm telling you."

Chase choked.

Tamra giggled from the doorway. "Hang in

65

there Sundance."

Struck dumb, he watched the door closed behind her. The traitor.

Between wishing she'd never mentioned his mother, relief the show fees were no longer an issue and worry over being able to pull this off with Chase as her subject, it had been a long night.

The 'Wild' campaign was centered on a contest to find the perfect man to represent the product. A lucrative contract for the winner and their agency was at stake so competition was stiff.

It was her job to take Chase and turn him into every woman's fantasy. Problem being, Chase had always been *her* fantasy.

Jerk, remember?

Oh, right.

After squeezing her little car in the last available space on the street, Jenna got out and looked around. He must not have come in yet. There was no sign of his big beast of a truck anywhere.

Mel was the only person she recognized when she got to the third floor and his smile was wide as she came through the door. "Morning Ms. Cordell."

"Please, call me Jenna. Ms. Cordell is too formal."

Mel reached out to shake her hand. "Okay, Jenna it is then. Now if you'll follow me, I'll show you where you'll be working today. Mr. Donavan is almost done in wardrobe so he should be along any time now."

Had she caught a snicker in Mel's voice? "Oh? I didn't see his truck outside, so assumed he wasn't here yet."

He did it again.

"What's so funny?"

Mel shrugged and waved her into one of the studio spaces. "Oh it's nothing really. Let's just say Georgie's idea of style and Mr. Donavan's I think differ to some degree."

"Georgie, who's Georgie?"

"He's one of our wardrobe mistresses." Mel winked. "His real name is George, but he prefers Georgina. We call him Georgie for short." Backing out of the room Mel stuck both thumbs up. "Cutting edge in fashion sense that one. In this biz it's all about pushing the limits, and boy, does he." Mel winked. "Between you and me, I'm thinking western wear will never be the same. Anyway, if there's anything you need, just holler."

"Thank you." Turning her attention to the studio Jenna took stock of her work area.

A fortune in equipment was at her disposal, from cameras to lighting, it was all there. The only drawback she could see was the backdrop they'd set up. It was supposed to be the inside of a barn but to her eye it was cliché and generic. Lighting it without completely washing it out was going to be a challenge.

Jenna started examining some of the camera accessories. Maybe she could do something with a filter, or try blurring it intentionally for a diffused effect. If she used a warm light and spot umbrella on Chase it might work.

Bang! The door flew open and hit the wall.

Jenna jumped fumbling the lens in her hand and barely caught it before it hit the ground. She looked up to find Chase standing in the doorway and was stunned into silence.

"Not. One. Word."

She started to laugh so hard she couldn't have uttered a word if she'd wanted to. Except for the highly polished red boots and the equally red sparkling band around his hat, everything was white. He was practically glowing and never in her life had she seen so many fringes.

The harder she laughed the more his expression shifted from pained to murderous. "Jenna."

Her name came out with a growl which did nothing for her self control. But knowing how out of his comfort zone Chase was, she didn't want to make it worse so she wiped the tears from her face and did her best to not hiccup. "Oh Chase, it's not that bad."

Chase reached back with his foot and kicked the door shut giving her a better look at his boots and it was all she could do to hold back another laughing fit. Was that chrome on the heels and toes?

"Not that bad!" He spread his arms wide showing off the extra long fringes, looked at her like she lost her mind and repeated himself in a voice an octave above normal. "Not that bad! I look like Howdy Doody from hell!" Reaching down Chase grabbed the legs of his white pleather chaps by even more fringes and yanked the legs aside, exposing the rhinestone studding decorating the top of his boots. "They're red and sparkle for chrissake!"

She noticed his face was nearly the same shade and Jenna sobered as she stepped closer to him and reached out to gently press his arms back down to his sides. "Yes, they are. But you having a coronary over it won't help anything."

A vein peeking out from under the brim of his sequin-banded ten gallon hat still throbbed and his wide eyes seemed more tinged with panic now than anger. Another of the heart strings she'd worked so hard to keep tethered yesterday went out to him and her hands slipped down his forearms to wrap around his clenched fists.

"Settle down Chase, I'll talk to Tamra and see it we can do something about—" Her voice trailed off as she took in the broad expanse of chest on display before her. He'd always been in good shape having worked on a ranch all his life, but now Chase's build had filled out and was more defined. It was all she could do not to reach up and run her fingers over all his slabs and abs.

Realizing where her mind had gone, Jenna pulled it out of the gutter and glanced up at his face, she knew she'd been caught by the heated look she found there.

Chase slipped his hands free of hers and broke the spell. "I don't think that'll do much good either. Tinkerbelle got a kick out of locking me away with Georgie."

"Tinkerbelle?"

For the first time since stepping into the room a ghost of a smile crossed Chase's face. "Yeah, Tamra, I call her that to get a rise out of her."

Jenna stomped a wave of jealousy into submission and wiped her hands on her pants to help unfurl her fists. What business was it of hers if he liked the shrimp?

His almost-smile broke into a dangerous lopsided grin. Wondering if he'd flashed that at Tamra earlier too, Jenna suddenly wanted to wipe that look off his face and give Shorty's ponytail a good yank.

Stuffing her inner fourteen year old back in the corner Jenna headed for the door and thankfully Chase moved out her way. "I'll go talk to this Georgie person and see if I can persuade him to see things more our way."

"Good luck." He grabbed her fingers and goose-bumps erupted on her arms. "I really mean that. If you can do something to get me out of this get up, I'll be forever in your debt."

She pictured helping him out of that get up personally and had an immediate urge to yank on her own hair as she shot out the door.

~*~*~

It had taken some doing, but Jenna managed to get Georgie to agree, jeans and a plaid shirt were more in keeping with the image Marla was looking for, than fringes and sequins; but only if the sleeves were ripped off the shirt and it was left open.

The sparkly hat was replaced with a straw one, but Georgie wouldn't budge on the chin strap. Chase still balked at the neck bandana but not nearly as much as the hip holster and fake gun. Some cajoling on her part and a pair of real leather chaps to replace the others, and he eventually decided it was 'less-worse' than the previous get up.

With the wardrobe issues finally settled Jenna discovered as long as she concentrated on lighting and photography rather than obsessing over her subject she was able to focus.

The camera responded instantly to Chase's good looks and innate charm more than making up for his lack of modeling experience. Once Jenna was able to get him chatting about the ranch, particularly his horses and JT, he relaxed and the flow became very natural which made for a productive morning of shooting in the studio.

But Jenna still wasn't getting what she wanted, so suggested a field trip. Chase, eager to be anywhere Georgie and his fringes were not, agreed whole-heartedly.

The outer cage to the elevator clanged shut as the thing lurched into motion. Chase cupped her elbow to steady her without losing a beat. "With Moon Dancer's nose damn near resting on top of JT's hat I had a hell of a time not busting a gut, which, needless to say, wouldn't have been in my best interest at the time."

Jenna rubbed the spot where his fingers had lingered a little longer than necessary. "I imagine it wouldn't. It's been a while, but I do remember JT's temper. It used to kill me how such a little guy could make you and your big bad brother toe-the-line."

Jenna caught the flicker of sadness on Chase's face and wanted to kick herself. First she reminds him of his mother's death, now his brother's. She may not want to allow herself to become involved with Chase again, but she certainly didn't want to cause him any undo pain either.

"Listen, Chase, I'm sorry. I shouldn't have—"

"No, it's okay. Ryan's gone and there's nothing anyone can do about it. So don't feel bad about mentioning him. Sometimes it helps to remember the good times, you know?"

"I suppose. But, I'm still sorry for yesterday...mentioning your mom."

Chase tipped his head so she couldn't see his face clearly, but she heard the minor quake in his voice. "That one's a little too fresh yet, so if you don't mind, I'd rather not talk about it." His fingers brushed hers for just a moment and she wanted to grab on. "But that doesn't excuse my snapping at you yesterday. How were you supposed to know?"

He pulled back to shove his hands in his pockets, like he always had when he was uncomfortable, and her chance slipped away. "What I'm not saying very well is that it's me who should apologize, not you."

Damn it. Where was the jerk when she needed him? Feeling the remorse pouring off him, Jenna cleared her throat of the lump forming against her will and gave in, placing her hand on his cheek. "I'm still sorry. And I'll try not to mention anything again unless you decide you want to talk about it. Okay?"

He closed his eyes and nuzzled into her hand wreaking havoc on the nerves in the centre of her palm and the remainder of her common sense.

"Thanks Jen."

Jenna pushed up on her toes to bring her lips in

line with his when the elevator bell announced their arrival in the lobby. Shocked at what she'd been about to do, her eyes snapped to his and she noticed the amused glint in his eye. Damn, he knew. She had to quit doing that.

Pulling her frayed dignity together she did her best to ignore the heat coming off him as she brushed by. "So, uh, JT; think he'll mind us taking some shots out at the ranch?"

"Last thing I want is for that old fart to catch wind of this."

Jenna suddenly remembered the two of them sneaking around the back of the barn while JT constantly looked over his shoulder and scratched the bald spot under his hat. She smiled. "How are we going to pull that off? He may have aged but I don't think enough to miss the camera flash going off."

"Nope, he wouldn't, that's why we're not going to the ranch; we're going up Coyote pass to Ribbon Valley instead."

"Your mom's land?"

"Uh huh, no one will bother us up there." Standing at the curb, Chase lifted his arm to block the sun from his eyes and scanned left and right. "What the...? Where's my truck?"

Jenna looked up and down the street but didn't spot any monster sized 4x4 anywhere. "I don't know. I didn't see it when I got here this morning. Where did you park?"

His tanned face took on a green tinge and he pointed. "Right there across the street, there was no room anywhere else."

A big blue sign was attached to a loading bay door directly across from where they stood. "Uh, Chase. Didn't you see the 'No Parking' sign?"

"Of course I did. But they didn't bother with it yesterday so I figured with today being Saturday it should be okay." He flung his arms out to the sides pointing both directions at once. "Besides, where the hell's a man supposed to park a real vehicle around here anyway?" He punctuated his claim with a stomp of his right boot.

He looked for all the world like a little boy whose favorite toy had been taken away and Jenna found herself again torn between sympathy for his situation and an insatiable need to laugh.

Deciding it was safer to avoid both, she bought herself a reprieve by burying her face in her bag to fish out her keys. "Being lunch time, chances of getting your truck back out of impound and still getting what we need done today is slim to none. It looks like we'll have to take my car out there, and pick up your truck when we're done."

"What if it wasn't towed? What if someone stole it?"

Jenna's hand froze on her keys. He could be right, and knowing there's no way Chase would be modeling if he didn't need the money; it also dawned on her, his truck wasn't only his ride, living on a ranch it was a huge part of his livelihood.

"Oh Chase, I'm sorry, I wasn't thinking. You need to call the police and ask if they have record of it being picked up. If they do you can find out how much money it'll take to bail it out, and if they don't, you'll need to report it stolen right away."

He didn't respond other than to clench his jaw and close his eyes tight.

"Chase? You have to call them."

He bent his head down and reached up to rub the back of his neck. "I cn. Foen wz in eye trik."

Jenna bent down and looked under the brim of his hat. "What?" His jaw was clamped down so tight it had to hurt. "You know I could understand you much better if your teeth weren't all clenched up like that."

The hand from his neck moved around to wipe his face and he blew out a puff of air. "I can't. My

77

phone was in my truck."

Without taking her eyes off him, Jenna slowly released her keys and wrapped her fingers around her phone. Pulling it out of her bag slowly she held it out under his nose. "I think we can make do with this one."

He looked at it and took a step back as though it might bite. "What's that?"

"My phone."

He planted his feet, crossed his arms and frowned. "It's pink."

Jenna's jaw dropped. This was no time for him to get stubborn and dig in his heels. They had to worry about Marla's tight deadline, his truck had been towed or worse, stolen, and all he can think about is the fact her phone is pink? "Are you kidding?"

"Yes." With the thundercloud frown on his face, it took a moment for what he'd said to register and when it did, her reaction was automatic.

She swung her purse at his head.

He ducked in the nick of time. "Hey! You could hurt someone with that you know."

"That's the general idea."

"Of course I was kidding. But after the morning I've had, you offer me a pink phone. What was I supposed to do? Let an opportunity like that pass? You should know me better than that by now." He plucked the phone from her hand and walked far enough away to allow pacing room.

His long legged gait held her attention and her ears tuned to the sound of his voice. All morning, things between them had felt easy like they had before the accident. How she wished it could be like that again.

Keeping a rein on her feelings was working about as well as herding cats.

You should know me better than that by now.

Jenna dragged a different memory out of the dark, the one of Chase ordering her out of his hospital room and out of his life.

She forced her eyes down and concentrated on how the sun glinted off her cherry red toenail polish. "Yes, I guess I should."

Now if only she could convince her heart and hormones to get with the program.

Chapter 6

"Okay, not sure if this is good news or not, but the police confirmed they did tow my truck this morning. It's in the Manchester impound lot and I can't get it out till morning."

Chase stepped in front of where Jenna sat and waited for her to lift her head. It hadn't dawned on him until it was too late where she'd end up looking.

He watched in frozen fascination as things slowed to a crawl and she focused on the area of denim directly below his belt buckle; an area currently swelling in direct proportion to the widening of her eyes and the rising heat in her cheeks.

"Jenna, honey, you keep looking at me there like that, and I may end up doing something about it that could land us in jail alongside my truck."

"Oh!"

She tried to scuttle backward but didn't make it far before Chase had her by the arms and lifted her to her feet. Only a few inches separated them and he wanted very much to pull her tight to his chest and close the gap and if she hadn't started to squirm he would have.

"Did I say I needed help? I'm perfectly capable of getting up on my own thank you." The way she absently stroked her arms where he'd had hold of her took the sting out of her words. She never could hide her feelings from him.

"Easy Jen, I just didn't want you to slip and hit your head. There are enough cracks in the sidewalk already."

The flustered pink in her cheeks rose and she started to sputter. "You...you...of all the...."

Chase started to chuckle and if he hadn't caught her mid charge they'd have ended up sprawled in the street. Before his common sense got in the way again he pulled her close, like he'd wanted to a moment earlier, relishing the way her soft curves instantly aligned to his larger frame. God, he'd missed this. No one else had ever felt as good or right as Jenna.

She sucked in a gasp through her soft lips and his, like bees to honey, were drawn to them. Their breath mingled and her eyelids fluttered closed. She smelled as fresh as spring, and he wanted to savour it.

"You better be helping her get an eyelash out of her eye Mr. Donavan."

They sprang apart and turned toward Marla,

81

whose scowl looked a lot like their tenth grade math teacher's when she'd caught them doing the same thing.

Jenna started to blink repeatedly. "I think you got it Chase. Thank you."

She was as cute now trying not to look guilty as she had then, and it was all he could do to keep a straight face. "Ah, that's good. Glad to help."

Marla's lip twitched and she gave them each a head to toe once over that had Chase sticking his hands in his pockets. "Oh, I should probably point out, in your contracts, there's a clause governing the conduct expected of our associates at 'Models to Go' - it's on page three. I suggest you acquaint yourselves with it before engaging in any more public displays of *helpfulness*. Capice?"

"Yes Ma'am."

Jenna didn't have pockets so clutched her purse in front of her. "Absolutely, I'll be sure to look it up."

Marla's lip twitched higher this time and on both sides. "Wonderful. Now that we're all on the same page, I'll get to why I was hoping to catch you before you left." Moving between them, she locked elbows with both. "What are you driving, by the way?"

Jenna gestured to her little tin can and Marla steered them toward it. "I took a quick look at your shots from this morning and love the potential there. I know I said you had a few days, but, now that I know Jenna can deliver and Chase is as good on film as I thought he'd be, I'd like to up the schedule."

"Up the schedule? But—"

"Not to worry you still have the rest of today and tomorrow."

Chase sensed Jen's rising panic right through the Marla barrier between them. "Ms. Gibson—"

"Uh, uh."

"I mean Marla, you sure that's a good idea? Jen and I are just starting to get into the swing of things."

Marla smirked but continued to look ahead. "I could see that for myself handsome, but in spite of that, I'm confident you two will deliver. In fact I confirmed with the client this morning that the final judging will be done during the Stampede this year, which we were already sure of. However, what we weren't aware of until now is that each agency will be submitting the name of another industry professional to be on the panel doing the judging."

Jenna's brow furled. "I'm sorry, but I don't

understand how this impacts our schedule."

"Of course you don't, because I haven't got to that yet." Having reached the car, Marla released their arms and turned to face them. "There's only one person I could trust to put forward for the job and luckily, I was able to reach her the minute I found out about this and she's agreed to do it." She held her hand out to quell any questions. "But, there's a catch."

She paused for so long, if Chase hadn't been raised a gentleman, he'd have shook it out of her. Thankfully Jenna prodded her before his fists blew out the bottom out of his pockets.

"She's a top photographer from across the pond I met a few years ago in Toronto during Fashion Week. The long flight from London will be to our advantage. If we get our final shot in her hands before she boards that plane, ours will be upper most in her mind because she won't even see the other entries until she arrives."

Jen seemed to get the significance even if Chase didn't. "Okay, so who is it?"

Marla posed her hands like a movie director framing a shot. "None other than Trisha Parker."

Chase's head was starting to spin. "Who?"

Both Jenna and Marla looked at him like he'd

grown a horn on his forehead and answered in stereo. "*The* photographer to the stars; the Shutter Queen herself, that's who."

Chase pulled the front of his hat down to block their glares and groaned. Oh, well that cleared things right up.

Not!

The beautiful, unspoiled stretch of land between the ranch and Ribbon Valley was some of the most deceiving and unruly kind of terrain in the Rockies. Filled with hungry muskeg bogs and treacherous rocks, eager to chew a hole in some unsuspecting low-slung gas tank, there was a good reason most traversed it on horseback or by four-wheel drive.

Something Jenna had dismissed out-of-hand after he suggested postponing this little venture until he had his truck back.

The trip up hadn't proven him wrong and after banging his head on the roof several times during it, Chase had to realign his joints before he could open the passenger door and unfold his body to get out. It occurred to him he was spending a lot of time lately with his knees kissing his ears and he didn't like it.

Once he'd pried himself loose and was standing he looked at the ground and grimaced. "Uh, Jen? Looks a little soft here."

"Chase for heaven's sake, I grew up around here too, you know. It's a little car not a tank like you drive. It'll be fine, now come on I don't want to loose the light."

"Fine, have it your way, but don't blame me if we get back and its little tires have sunk past their rims."

"Quit being such a worry-wart." She'd snagged the camera bag and tripod, leaving the small portable generator and heavier duffel bag full of lighting stuff for him. "Grab those will you, and come on."

"Oh I get it, so driving, you're the guy. But carrying the heavy stuff, I am. I see."

"Bit sexist, but it works for me, now quit grumbling and hurry up."

"I don't grumble."

The sound of her laughter drifted back to him on the summer breeze and his insides did a funny flip-flop. *Careful Chase, you don't want to go there.*

Why not?

Because the only way she's interested in seeing

you is through her camera lens. You made sure of that four years ago, remember? Besides, in a day or two this will all be over, you'll go your separate ways again and that'll be that.

Didn't mean he couldn't enjoy the view in the mean time. Hefting the bag over his shoulder Chase sprinted after her taking particular note of the way her jeans hugged her shapely backside as she broke through the trees and reached the top.

"Chase, you've got to see this. The view is spectacular."

Busy admiring the curves ahead, Chase couldn't agree more.

A weight that had nothing to do with the equipment bag settled over him and it took longer to shake it loose this time. He'd have to be more careful where his mind wandered.

When he caught up, Jenna was standing completely still on the crest of the bluff staring down into the deeper valley below, hidden from view until now.

The pine and cottonwood trees they'd dodged climbing to this point, now gave way to a blue spruce and aspen blanket covering the sides of a deep bowl. Surrounded by soaring peaks, a sparkling lake lay cradled at the bottom; its

87

turquoise color unique to high-mountain passes like this one.

"I'd forgotten how beautiful it is."

Chase dropped his shoulder and let the duffel bag slide down his arm to rest on the ground next to Jenna's equipment. There was no relief from the summer heat even this high up, so he slipped his shirt off and used it like a towel to wipe his hands and face then tied it around his waist as he moved to the edge next to her. "I know. When I was a kid I didn't get what was so special about this place. To me it was just another valley." He felt more than saw her turn toward him. "It wasn't until I was older and everyone started to have a conniption fit over resort developers sniffing around that I started to see it with new eyes."

"Is that why your dad bought it?"

"Partly." Chase reached down, picked up a pebble and rolled it between his fingers. "But really, I think it was his last attempt to get on the good side of my grandfather. This was always sacred land to Mom's family, which is why Dad put it solely in her name."

"I wasn't very old at the time, but I do remember bits and pieces about that. What was that about again, something to do with ribbons and trees?"

"Prayer Ribbons; tied to a tree branch so they flutter. The People believe prayers continually carried on the wind this way will be heard and answered."

"Do they still do that?"

Chase hesitated before answering and tossed his stone out over the valley. "Far as I know." As he watched it disappear into the trees, a specter of his childhood beliefs stirred deep down.

If he'd said a prayer and tied a ribbon for his mother, would it have been heard and answered?

A twig snapped behind them distracting him from the thought and Chase caught a familiar scent on the wind. He touched Jenna's arm lightly to get her attention and raised his finger to his lips. She frowned and gave him a look like he'd lost his senses, but she held still.

Another snap confirmed what Chase suspected. At the moment, they were downwind so their visitor hadn't sensed them yet.

A shiver of excitement zinged under his skin and he caught himself holding his breath. He'd experienced something similar as a boy and knew if he and Jenna were very careful, she too might have a chance to see something only a privileged few ever did.

Crouching slowly he guided Jenna to do the same and pointed where he wanted her to look, all the while listening for further movement in the trees.

Soon his patience was rewarded with the heavy tread of something big moving through the brush near-by. Jenna shifted closer and slipped her hand in his.

A trio of snorts came first, then a velvet nose held high in the air sensing for danger poked past the brush followed by a black head and flowing mane. A tiny gasp escaped Jenna and she locked her grip on his hand so tight his knuckles collided.

The mustang stallion swung his head and spotted them. Chase sensed the excitement rising in Jenna and willed her to stay motionless. If the horse spooked they wouldn't get a second chance.

The animal lifted his head again but this time when he blew through his nostrils the vibration from his vocal cords was missing. Chase smiled and wiggled his hand till his palm met Jenna's. The stallion's blow signaled he'd gone from wary to curious.

His ears twitched and his nostrils flared in and

out a few times, then he shifted to the side dismissing them and leaned down to chew on the tender grass under his hooves.

His coat was shaggier than his domestic counterparts but Chase could still make out the shadowy markings sprinkled across his hindquarters. Dappling was as individual to a horse as finger prints to a human, and this one's zigzag blotches resembled a lighting bolt.

A flutter tickled his belly and woke the boy he thought lived only in the old family photo, filling him with wonder. Hot damn! Chase knew this guy.

His cousin, Cohen, had christened him Thunderhead, not because of the marking, but because the animal was stubborn as a mule. Cohen was famous for his way with all animals, most usually walked right up and stuck their noses in his hand.

Not Thunderhead. It had taken the man years of courting the beast before it allowed Cohen to finally touch him.

Chase spent two summers traipsing through the back country with his cousin after that and had encountered the wild herd several times. Cohen even managed to get the mustang to tolerate Chase's touch by the end of the second season.

Wondering if the horse would remember him too, Chase eased his hand out of Jenna's, signaling her to stay put, and crouching low, slowly made his way toward the clearing.

Keeping his hands down by his sides and slightly cupped with the palms out, Chase spoke quietly in a low soothing monotone as he approached Thunderhead the way Cohen had taught him as a boy. Knowing the stallion was the herd's alpha Chase was careful to come in from the side and concentrated on not making direct eye contact. The last thing Chase wanted to convey was any kind of challenge.

Within six feet Thunderhead's ears swiveled, and he nickered a cautious hello, but otherwise held his position.

At about the two foot mark, he blew again and shifted his back end a hair. Attune to every minuscule muscle movement on the animal's part, Chase's heart pounded in his chest, and a bead of sweat trickled down his spine. Thunder could still spook so he kept the sound of his voice consistent and slowly brought his hand in under his nostrils.

Thunder's next blow was softer and the muscles on his neck twitched as though shaking off a fly, then he bent his head for a sniff.

His sniff turned to a tooth-shielded nip which quickly became a lip-nibbling session all the way up Chase's arm. As attuned as he was to the mustang he was also aware of Jenna's camera shutter softly clicking like mad behind him.

Hoping he'd be able to see her without disturbing the balance he'd achieved with Thunderhead, Chase turned his head so he could look over his left shoulder and felt the horse's breath warm his skin as his regal head came over his right.

Jenna was where he'd left her, and even if her face was mostly hidden behind the camera, he could see it was flushed and split in a mile-wide grin.

With Thunder's chin rubbing his back Chase took a chance and raised his arms till they loosely circled the massive neck so he could scratch under his mane. Beyond them the sun's rays split as it fell behind the trees, burnishing the meadow and lighting the cottonwood fluff floating by to a soft glow.

Chase had come close to heaven once before, in the arms of the woman behind him. Having her here, now, to share this experience was a damn close second. Wanting to hold onto the peace flowing over him, Chase closed his eyes and took in the heightened sounds and smells around him.

The horse's musk, the sweet grass mixed with pine and a hint of Jenna's perfume. He wanted it filed away with the rest when today was but a memory.

Lost as he was in a cocoon of past nostalgia and present harmony, he never saw it coming and didn't stand a chance.

Chapter 7

On instinct alone Jenna managed to slip her camera out. As nervous as she was for Chase, she needed to record this once in a lifetime moment, preferably before she forgot what her lungs were for, something she should probably remind herself how to use right now.

After all, how could she kill him for scaring the daylights out of her if she was on the ground in a dead faint from lack of oxygen?

Good grief! Was he nuts? He may have native roots on his mother's side and know more about animals than most, but honestly, what man in his right mind waltzed up to a wild horse like that?

It was insane...unbelievable...magical.

The play of muscles flowing under the smooth skin of Chase's bare back and the ripple of light playing over the stallion's black coat needed to be immortalized.

She'd knock some sense into him after.

As quietly as possible she expanded her protesting lungs then slowly released everything down to her diaphragm, and lifted the camera into position. A brief pause to set and Jenna started shooting as fast as the camera would let her.

Through the viewfinder she saw Chase turn his head her way as the horse's head come over his opposite shoulder. The angle of the sun brought Chase's arms into stark definition as he lifted them and haloed both his, and the mustang's, dark heads. Her finger continuously pressed the shutter button as a gentle gust of wind lifted the stallion's mane and toyed with it while Chase leaned in and closed his eyes.

The light and composition were perfect. Jenna smiled so wide her cheeks tingled and every part of her being zeroed in on capturing this one perfect image.

Suddenly a rifle report bounced through the valley and shattered everything, turning the magic moment into instant mayhem.

Jenna dropped the camera and clenched her fists over her ears. Before she registered what the noise had been the stallion reared up, the whites of its eyes visible as he pedaled his forelegs in the air and screamed his indignation.

His flailing hooves crashed down hard enough to send a tremor through the meadow taking Chase down with them. He vanished under the dust storm the enraged animal's hooves churned up, firing Jenna's heart into her throat.

"Chase!"

She charged straight for them waving her arms in the air, her primal scream blending with the mustang's as he wheeled away and vanished into the trees.

Closing the gap to where she thought he went down Jenna's eyes darted over the scene and through the settling cloud and picked out his prone figure.

He wasn't moving.

Memory merged with nightmares, past melded with present, and the fragile rein holding back the full onslaught of panic snapped. "No!"

The meadow blurred, becoming a rodeo infield. The blood pounding in her ears became the roar of the crowd. Stumbling, she tripped on a root and landed hard, scraping her hands without feeling a thing. How could it be happening again?

Her vision blurred. It was easier to crawl the last bit, until her palm connected with solid muscle and warm skin. Choking on tears she prayed.

"Oh God, please, no."

Her hands skimmed the surface of his arm from wrist to shoulder. Registering no protruding bones or sticky blood helped anchor her. Okay, good. Repeating the process on the other side gave the same result and her brain started to function again. She needed to check for a pulse then check for swelling.

Chase winced and moaned as Jenna pressed her fingertips next to his Adam's apple, startling her. He was alive! Relief took over her tear ducts and if she hadn't been concerned about the possibility of internal injuries she'd have pounced on his beautiful chest.

Jenna tipped her head back and took a swipe at her face trying to banish the dust laden tears from her sight and whispered. "Thank you God." Bracing herself, she leaned over and gingerly cupped his cheek. "Chase? Can you hear me?" When he didn't respond she brushed the hair from his forehead and spoke louder. "Baby, come on talk to me. You need to tell me what hurts."

His brow wrinkled and his eye lids fluttered as he gulped like a fish out of water until he was finally able to suck in labored breath.

Okay, he was breathing. That was good.

He stuck one hand behind his head, covered his eyes with the other and moaned again.

Oh, no. He must have hit it or been kicked. She had to keep him from moving. "Chase, you need to stay still for a minute. Don't move your head.

Where does it hurt?"

He tipped his hand up enough she could see his eyes were cracked open.

"I think...maybe...."

"Yes?"

"It's...my pride."

His voice was raspy but he did appear to be able to focus on her...Jenna's mind tripped mid-thought. Wait a minute? "Your what?"

"My pride." He took in another good helping of air and ended up with a coughing fit for his trouble. "Pretty sure it's terminal."

Once his breathing was back under control, Jenna sat back and narrowed her eyes. "You hurt your pride?"

He nodded.

"That's all? Everything else is okay?"

"Uh huh."

She wiped her hands on her thighs, drying the residual tears and curled them into fists. "You're sure? No pain in your arms or shoulders or anything?"

He shook his head. "No."

"Positive?"

"Yah."

"Good." Jenna cocked her arm back and

punched him in the shoulder as hard as she could.

"Hey!" What was that for?"

"Chase Donavan, you jerk! You scare the life out of me, send me into fits and all you did was mangle your big fat male ego!"

Chase's lip started to quiver.

She thought the horse had saved her the trouble of knocking him senseless, but apparently it hadn't done a darn bit of good. Didn't he know this was serious? "You're positive? What about ringing in your ears?"

"Only your melodious voice."

She growled and resisted the urge to punch him again. Even to her, her voice was anything but melodious at the moment. "What about your ribs any pain when you breathe?"

"Jen, really, I'm okay—"

The more Chase tried to convince her he was fine, the more her tone turned surly and filled with sarcasm, but she couldn't help it. "What about your other side, tough guy? Maybe I should give it a shot too. Lord knows you deserve it."

Chase tossed her a lopsided grin that normally would've turned her resolve to jelly and pushed himself up on one elbow.

Spoiled brat, if he thought a little sugar was

going to get him out of this one, he had another thing coming.

His smile stretched and little sparks of mischief flickered in his eyes as he leaned the other shoulder toward her and winked. "Come on, slugger. If it'll make you feel better, go ahead. Give it your best shot."

Great, now he looked completely adorable...not to mention edible.

His hair had slipped its tie to fall in a messy tangle of dark waves and without his shirt on, his shoulders supporting his propped up position like that made her mouth water.

He's not yours anymore.

Maybe not, but she couldn't stand the thought of a world without him somewhere in it. Why couldn't he see he might've been killed just now? Desperate for him to realize taking risks like that was no laughing matter, Jenna's mouth kicked in before getting the all clear from her brain.

"What about your legs, can you move them?"

As soon as the words passed her lips, Chase blanched and she wished she could snatch them back.

~*~*~

His legs! Bolting the rest of the way upright, Chase grabbed his legs and fired mental commands at his muscles to move. It took a moment for his adrenaline flooded brain to acknowledge they'd answered. He broke into a cold sweat and wiggled his toes in his boots, bent his knees and rotated his hips; he hadn't lost anything. Not even the sharp twinge in his lower back. For the first time he was thankful for that.

His chin dropped to his chest with a sigh. A tremor ran through his body shedding some of the tension, but not all. His fears may have been set aside, but not the anger, or the hurt. Chase couldn't believe what just came out of her mouth, but better to keep his own shut than say something he'd regret.

Like before, when you told her to leave and not look back?

He rolled to his side and shot to his feet.

"Chase wait, I—"

He stormed off in the direction of his nose. Damn it. How could she say that to him? They may not be together anymore, but she of all people knew what he'd been through. Hell she'd been close enough to hear his back snap when the wagon barreled over him that day.

Yes, but you ran her off, so she never saw what you went through to come back from that.

Besides, when Thunderhead plowed him down, it wasn't like he hadn't had a heart attack, too. He'd eaten his lungs for lunch and nearly needed to change his pants, for chrissake!

After the grooming from hell, his truck gets towed, stupid poachers are shooting up his land again, he's nearly trampled and now Jenna winds up and hits him below the belt. Whose bloody cornflakes had he pissed in this morning? That's what he wanted to know.

Through the mire of his temper Chase knew Jenna was right behind him. She was as stubborn as ever and why did she have to make everything out to be such a big deal? What happened today had been scary for a minute, sure, but it hadn't been that bad.

Had it?

He remembered hearing the gun shot. Then Thunder's neck muscles bunching as the underside of the stallion's massive jaw flew over Chase's head; the weird sensation of suspended time, as all that unleashed power surged, breaking the circle of Chase's arms, and exploded toward the sky. Then the sheer terror, as those scissoring hooves came straight at him.

Okay, there was that.

"Chase, wait. Would you slow down?"

He growled. Why should he? A sliver of guilt niggled at his conscience but he choked it into submission.

He had a right to be mad, damn it.

How he'd managed to dive out of the way and not get trampled today, he'd never know. All he remembered was hitting his head, eating dirt, and pulling his arms up to protect his face as he started to roll. Then nothing until he heard Jen calling him. Sure it could've been worse, but the point was it hadn't been.

"Chase! Please. I'm sorry."

He wasn't going to listen to this, so she might as well give up.

"I thought you were really hurt, then you weren't and you laughed."

So, what? She'd rather he'd been banged up and cried like a baby?

"I wanted you to see how serious things could've been. But as usual you wouldn't quit joking around. I was so mad...and scared...I didn't think about what I was saying!"

She was closing the gap, so he lengthened his stride. Couldn't she take a hint? And what did she mean as usual?

The rustle of grass behind him stopped, and her voice shook.

"Damn it, Chase! It was like the infield crash all over again, all right. I'm sorry. But *you* didn't have to stand by helpless and watch it happen all over again."

Chase own steps slowed and stopped.

"What if that had been me just now? Would *you* have laughed it off if the shoe were on the other foot?"

Chase's guts twisted. What if it had been Jen on the ground under Thunder's hooves instead of him?

His imagination supplied a play by play from her perspective, both of today and the day of his crash at the Stampede. His head fell forward and he closed his eyes, forcing his throat to swallow the bitter pill.

Chase, you ass. You were so busy feeling sorry for yourself, you never gave a moment's thought to what anyone else, particularly Jenna, suffered. Did you?

How would he have handled her lying broken

and miserable in a hospital bed telling him to hit the hi-way? That it was over between them.

Like shit. That's how.

For the first time Chase understood what he'd put her through. He'd broken it off to give Jenna her freedom; to save her from a life of looking after half a man who could no longer walk. He'd even deluded himself into believing his sacrifice was noble.

But it had nothing to do with being noble, did it? No, it had everything to do with self-pity. Jenna trusted him with her heart and he'd thrown it aside in favor of pride.

He hadn't been selfless; he'd been selfish.

He had to admit he was being a jack-ass now because the last few days had shown him exactly what he'd tossed away, and in spite of everything, he wanted it back.

No. He wanted Jen back.

Yah, good luck with that buddy, let me know how that works out for you.

"Chase, please say something."

He turned around and his heart swelled; he'd been such a fool, simply looking at her stole his breath away. Her lips were parted and the lace edge of her shirt was quivering with each shallow breath she took. Her eyes appeared huge in her delicate face and shone with unshed tears. She looked like something out of a legend from his childhood, a forest spirit visible only because she chose to be, but ready to vanish in an instant.

Beautiful, delicate, vulnerable - *His.*

He wanted to take her in his arms and erase the past so badly his voice cracked. "Jen?"

A tear slipped from the corner of her eye and with a whimper she broke into a run. Chase opened his aching arms and caught her tight to his chest mid-launch.

"I'm...sorry...I—"

Peppering his face with kisses she stuttered between hiccups and clamped her legs around him.

Chase was busy with his own nips and licks, trailing them from the hollow of her collarbone to the tip of her ear. "Shhh, baby shhh."

"When...he reared...I—"

"No, shhh. It's me who should be sorry."

Jenna pressed down on his hipbones with her inner thighs, aligning the juncture of those mile long legs perfectly with the straining bulge behind his zipper, instantly setting him on fire.

"Chase, I didn't mean it like that...I would never...you know I didn't right?"

"I know. I'm sorry I was such an ass—"

Chase slid his hands from Jenna's slender waist so he could fill them with the soft curves he'd been admiring earlier and pressed her heated core closer still.

Her back arched and her head fell back exposing the long line of her throat lifting her chest within reach. He wasted no time accepting her invitation.

Dipping his head, Chase sucked in her intoxicating scent and nuzzled his face across the top of the silky mounds in front of him.

He could hardly believe he was touching her like this again. He'd spent more sleepless nights dreaming of her and waking up sporting a hard on because of it than he cared to admit.

His chin grazed the tight peak of her nipple and Chase squashed the little voice warning him to stop before things got any more out of control. Her soft gasp spurred him on and he pulled the tempting tip into his mouth, suckling her through her shirt. Her gasp rose to a moan and she buried her fingers in his hair.

"Oh God, Chase, I can't believe this is happening. I must be out of my mind."

His heart skipped and it took everything he had

to corral the hormones stampeding through his veins as he let his tender little morsel slip from his lips. Focusing in on the wet spot he'd made Chase prayed he wouldn't have to shove the randy little critters all the way back in the barn. "If you are, does that mean you want back in?"

When she didn't answer right away he wanted to bawl like a new born calf barred from its mother. Then Jenna fisted a chunk of his hair and gently tugged. "No. I don't."

Chase grinned and his hormones cheered. "Whew, good. Me neither."

Jenna giggled drawing his attention back to the peak visible through the damp material and another surge of blood raced to his groin making his jeans downright painful.

A desperate need to feel her bare skin next to his filled him and Chase's world tightened down to one immediate goal.

Get naked. Now.

Jenna' stomach flip-flopped at the predatory look on Chase's face. She was crazy to do this; she was opening herself up for a world of hurt afterward, but with him looking at her like he was a starving wolf and she was a juicy T-bone, how could she resist?

She'd been attracted to him when he was a gangly youth, now she was looking at a mature man. In her eyes, Chase was the epitome of masculine beauty and grace, all wrapped in sleek muscle and tawny skin. Every female nerve in her body screamed out for him; consequences be-damned.

All that power and intensity focused solely on her was intoxicating and her head was buzzing. He slowly dropped to his knees holding her like she was the most precious thing in the world and had both her heart and her reawakened girly bits gushing.

Chase settled her gently on her back then shifted till his butt was perched on his heels, trailing his hands down her arms and over her thighs, never once taking his gaze from hers. "Tell me this is what you want."

She knew how hard it was for him to ask. His eyes were soft but intense in the fading glow of sunset and she could see the huge bulge straining in his pants as he waited for her answer. His power and restraint, so beautiful and raw, words failed her.

So Jenna let her hands do the talking.

Still holding his gaze she started popping open the buttons down the front of her shirt. With each one, her breathing increased matching the rate of each inhale Chase pulled through his flared nostrils.

The last button slipped free and Jenna let the sides fall away. Like a magnet drawn to steel, Chase's eyes dropped and he swallowed hard. Jenna's nipples perked up higher, tingling and straining under the thin material of her bra. As he slowly rubbed his hands up and down her thighs she felt the tension build in the muscles of his where they flanked her.

On a rush of feminine power Jenna moved to undo the clasp of her bra but his hands came down over hers, stopping her. "No, let me."

Passion flared hot, dilating his pupils as he pushed the scrap of cloth out of his way and cupped her breasts, pressing them closer together and rolling his thumbs over the sensitized peaks. "You don't know how many times I've wanted to touch you like this in the last few days."

She'd caused the guttural quality of his voice. Relishing the thought, Jenna's nerves fired at random and her legs twitched. She wanted to drive him as senseless as he was her, so she wiggled closer and stroked his erection through the worn denim but it wasn't good enough. She needed the naked length and weight of him pulsing in her palm.

Chase dove forward and feasted on her aching breasts, momentarily throwing her off her goal, licking and nibbling first one nipple then the other. His silky hair tickled her and filled her head with a mixture of cologne and heated male flesh. The opposing rough texture of his day old beard and the moist velvet inside his mouth shut all but the most primal part of her down and Jenna went after Chase's straining zipper as though her life depended on getting in there.

"Yes." He growled as he brought his mouth down over hers, shifting one knee between hers and pressing in tight so she could rock against him.

She pushed his jeans over his hips and dragged the front of his shorts down. His penis sprang forward, the velvet tip leaving a trail of moisture across her belly.

Driving his tongue past her lips, Chase plundered the inside of Jenna's mouth as she shoved at the bunched up denim, further baring his ass.

Grabbing the taut cheeks, she dug in and held on as his hips pumped, rubbing against her and mirroring the thrusts of his tongue.

Chase braced his weight above her on one arm and angled his other hand between them, fumbling with her zipper. Yes, that's what she wanted. With her breath ragged and blood pounding in her ears, Jenna brushed his hand away and lifted off the ground enough to shimmy out of her own pants.

Chase broke their kiss with a nip on her bottom lip and dipped his hand inside her panties sliding the tip of his finger between her outer lips with ease. "So wet already."

He found the swollen nub hidden there and played her like an instrument while he nibbled on her ear lobe. "You feel so good Jen."

She curled her fingers around his penis and pumped her fist, gently squeezing the head on the way up and dragging moisture down the length on her way back, until he was slick and moving freely in her palm. Chase started to pant and buck his hips as his hand in turn delved deeper and he pressed two fingers inside her.

Jenna's back bowed and she clamped her thighs tight, riding his hand. "Chase, please."

"God, I want inside you so badly."

"Yes! Please, yes!"

Chase swooped in to claim her mouth again while they both fumbled and tugged until she was at

113

last free of her panties. Chase barely took the time to shove his own pants down to his knees before he was spreading her legs wide and settling himself between them.

Jenna tilted her hips up to receive him. "Now!"

Chase took hold of himself and brushed the tip of his penis between her folds adding a hint of pressure each time he met the flap of skin shrouding her swollen clitoris.

Jenna needed him to fill her so badly, she couldn't take it anymore. On his next down sweep she thrust her hips up and grabbed his ass to pull him in.

Their bodies joined like a well oiled lock and key and danced in perfect harmony to the rhythm of their rising passion.

Tuned to Chase's racing heart, undulating thrusts and building tension, Jenna rode the rising wave. "More, please Chase...more."

Of their own accord her legs curled up and circled over his back till her ankles locked and Chase's next thrust buried so deep she swore she hit her womb. "Oh yes...like that."

Chase hissed and his hips started to piston, every muscle in his arms and back straining. "Can't...stop." A low vibration started in his chest and Jenna's moans of pleasure increased with his pace. "Oh, Chase...go, go, go."

"Going to...come so...hard."

Chase's balls slapped against the sensitized skin behind her entrance adding fuel to the flames and robbing Jenna of the ability to do anything but hold on.

"Can't...stop."

He claimed her mouth in a frantic mating of lips and reached between them to press his thumb against her clitoris. Jenna's world exploded and she flew apart with it, hitching a ride to the sun on the shattered pieces.

She thrust her hips up and dug her heels into Chase's lower back, locking him deep and milked every pulse as he found his own release.

With the last ripples of pleasure still coursing between them, Chase slowly rocked his hips and stroked her from rib to knee, helping her relax her muscles and lower her legs. He scattered feather light kisses over her cheeks and flicked the top of his tongue on the end of her nose then along the line of her lips as he helped guide her gently back to earth. "You're amazing. Thank you."

"So are you, an...and you're welcome." She'd almost said 'anytime', but caught herself and kissed his brow as she cradled his head in her arms. She didn't want to say anything that would ruin their wonderful afterglow, but she could no longer ignore the question rolling around her head either. Could there still be a chance for them?

It was obvious they both still had strong feelings for each other and the chances Chase would take on modeling, unless he had no other choice, were slim.

Her mind fit the pieces together and a crack formed in the armor encasing her heart. It was the only thing that made sense. He had to have given up racing, otherwise he wouldn't need money so bad.

Jenna opened her eyes to a bold, bright moon shining down at them and she couldn't contain her smile. If Chase really had curbed his reckless streak, maybe they could try again.

She tossed the idea around for several minutes until she realized Chase had slowly grown heavier. She couldn't see his face so listened carefully and picked up the deep even cadence of his breathing. Her face broke into a giddy grin; poor man, she must have worn him out.

Jenna glided her hand over the silken length of his hair and down the corded muscle next to his spine. She'd let him sleep for a while. Wrapping her arms as far around him as she could, she nuzzled her cheek on the top of his head and tried to follow him into dreamland with no luck.

Try as she might, Jenna's mind insisted on crafting mental clips of the wonderful future her re-opened heart was already counting on.

Chapter 8

Any resemblance to the warm and willing woman he tickled awake with a piece of grass as the sun came up, then made love to two more times before hiking back out to the car, was gone.

As he'd feared, her little heap had sunk to its tin fenders in the soft ground which, to his surprise, Jenna had taken in stride. But then, he'd made the mistake of saying he'd told her so, which was why he was rubbing a sore arm now.

And she didn't look the least bit sorry either. Sitting there with her arms crossed, looking straight out the windshield. "It serves you right."

JT snickered and shifted to a lower gear as they climbed the last incline before heading down to the ranch. "She's right you know. Pointing out the obvious to a lady is like poking a rattler with a six inch stick. Just plain stupid."

Leaning past Jenna, Chase glared at JT. "Kinda like you laughing your ass off when I told you where we were and why?"

JT snorted. "You're just sore because you had to call me in the first place and I found out you got your truck police-napped."

Jenna stifled a giggle. "Now JT, Chase

would've told you about the truck."

"No, I wouldn't."

"See. Boy admits it."

"Chase!"

"I wouldn't. I knew if he found out, I'd never hear the end of it." Chase wrinkled his face and scratched his chin and produced a surprisingly good imitation to JT's higher voice. "Way I see it, you gotta be pretty dumb to go to the city in the first place, let alone park in a loading zone. Might as well stick a big sign on it; here come and get it, I dare ya!"

"Hmph, thought you were taught better than to disrespect your elders and that still doesn't excuse you for telling Jenna 'you told her so'. Don't blame her a bit for bopping you one."

They topped the ridge and hit a rut in the road bouncing all three in their seats. Jenna tipped forward and braced herself on Chase's thigh, and he instinctively reached his arm out in front of her, earning him a raised eyebrow from JT.

In response, Chase shot a warning look back the ranch hand had the good sense to heed.

Jenna snatched her hand away and blushed, reminding him of how she'd looked earlier flushed from head to toe after her last orgasm. His penis twitched in his pants, perking up at the thought, and Chase shifted the camera bag a little higher on his lap.

JT kept his eyes on the road in front of them and scratched his chin. "So we should be able to get back with tow chains and get your car out this afternoon."

Jenna's head turned at the sound of the camera bag rustling in Chase's lap and her eyes opened wider. "Oh. This afternoon." Her gaze snapped forward and she sucked her bottom lip in between her teeth. "That would be great."

The tips of Chase's ears flared hot. Shit, she knew. The insistent bulge under the bag jumped and got bigger as they were entering the main gate.

Damn it. They'd gone at it like bunnies twice in the last few hours and he couldn't get his mind off having her again as soon as possible. Sneaking his hand under the bag he pushed through the material to shift himself out from under the zipper.

Jenna released her lip then licked it.

An unbidden picture of Jenna knocking the bag to the floor, whipping his pants open, taking his penis in her mouth and working him over like an ice cream cone flashed in Chase's mind. It was all he could do to swallow a groan as the damn thing shot rock hard and started doing the two-step.

JT pulled up in front of the house and shut off the rattling engine. "Chase you've got a phone message in the house and I'm sure Jenna'd like to clean up some after being stuck in the woods with you all night."

A little gasp popped out of her and she went from a pretty pink to mottled red. "I...oh, that is—"

Chase had the sudden urge to plow JT for embarrassing her. "I'm sure she does." Banging the sticky door open with his shoulder, Chase slid out of his seat, making sure to keep the bag strategically placed and reached in to help Jenna out. "You can use my mom's room, you remember where it is?"

"Yes."

It irked him that she didn't look up and dropped his hand the minute her feet hit the ground. He watched her stiff back as she headed for the house. What exactly was she upset about; JT knowing they'd been together or the fact they had been? Chase had started thinking they might be able to get back together. Had he read her wrong?

And JT looking at him like Chase had been caught screwing his prom date in the back seat of her daddy's car wasn't improving his mood.

A boat of a Buick, lavender taffeta and velvet

pink thighs popped into Chase's head. Well, okay he had - Jenna had looked sexy in her prom dress but she'd been hotter than hell out of it - which was beside the point. They weren't seventeen anymore.

Chase glared at JT who returned a black look of his own and he pointed over his shoulder as he grumbled. "Guess I'll just mosey on over to the barn while you two tidy up. See if I can dig up those tow chains."

Chase grunted an acknowledgement then headed in after Jenna. By the time he clomped his way across the front porch his jaw hurt from grinding his teeth. He wanted some answers, and he was bloody well going to have them. If their being together had been nothing but a one time thing for her, he had a right to know about it.

Chase barged in the front door making the old lead glass in it rattle. "Jenna!"

She rolled around the corner from the kitchen, with her hand on her stomach and her eyes sparkling. "Hey there Black Bart." She bent over in a fit of laughter and slid down the wall until her butt hit the floor. "Oh my god, if you two could've seen your faces. It was all I could do to get in the house without busting a gut."

Chase's lower jaw met his chest.

"Oh Chase, I'm sorry." Her laughter disintegrated into a fit of giggles and tears started to roll down her face, "You both puffed up...like a pair of...cock-roosters."

A burp of laughter escaped Chase's throat, then another, and before he knew it, he was laughing out loud too. "I'm warning you, if you don't cut that out, I'll have to give you a reason to carry on like that."

Jenna giggled harder and flopped to her side gasping for air.

He dropped the bag, kicked the door shut behind him and started flexing his fingers with an evil grin on his face. "Okay, you asked for it."

Jenna squealed, jumped to her feet and scrambled down the hallway toward the bedrooms with Chase right on her heels.

Jenna woke to the sound of bees buzzing, a lilac scented breeze teasing the drapes covering the window and Chase's lips nuzzling her neck from behind.

"Hey, sleepy."

His fingers stroked in a gentle rhythm between

123

her legs and a tingle rippled the length of her kindling body. "Hey, yourself."

She blinked in the subdued late afternoon light surrounding them and stretched like a cat and smiled. He'd caught her before she reached his mother's old room and pulled her into his much closer one instead and she wasn't complaining.

Once they'd recognized their mutual attraction as teenagers the chemistry between them had always been there, but holy cow, nothing like the unbridled fire they had for each other now. She couldn't seem to get enough of him and if the hardening length pressing against the back of her thighs was any indication he couldn't get enough of her either.

Chase pressed two fingers deep inside her and his thumb took over circling her clitoris picking up the pace. "You drive me crazy woman."

Jenna's hips started dancing to his tune of their own accord and her toes clenched over his. "Back at ya, Bart."

In one motion Chase pulled away, and spun her toward him, dragging her on top so she straddled him. Grabbing her behind the knees he adjusted her until she was planted on top of his erection and looking at his face. "Bart?" Grasping her hand, he led her fingers toward him and lifted his hips, making room for her to do the guiding to her opening.

Glad to comply Jenna wrapped her fingers around him and circled her thumb over the weeping tip while slowly pumping his length as she eased him inside her equally wet entrance. Loving the way he filled her, she tipped her head back and her eyelids fluttered. "Bart...Chase...oooh, same thing."

"Look at me," Chase growled. His fingers dug into her hips, almost to the point of pain, and he stopped moving beneath her.

"Jenna. Look. At. Me."

Hearing the tone change in his voice she blinked her eyes open and a tiny alarm bell went off in her head. Stark possession was stamped all over his face.

"I want you to know who's inside you when you come." His hips bucked, lifting her so he could take over the ride from below.

Where was this coming from? "Chase—"

"Look at me. Watch my face."

Wrapping his arms around her, Chase rolled, pinning her beneath him. He trapped her hands above her head but his voice softened easing her worry. "Don't look away."

With her attention where he wanted it, his grip where he held her wrists gentled. His hips started to rock back and forth stroking her right where her body screamed for release. "Stay with me."

Like she had a choice. Her rising need robbed her of the ability to do anything else.

Chase released her wrists in favor of her butt and Jenna wrapped her legs around him, matching thrust for thrust never tearing her gaze from his. Not even when she exploded inside sending wave after wave of ecstasy crashing through her. "Chase!"

He blanketed her, capturing her mouth with his, swallowing her moans of pleasure as he tensed and pulled her tight to him. His throat rumbled with his own release and her body took all he had to give as they sailed over the edge together.

As she floated back to earth, Jenna wasn't sure if her heart or her ears heard the words 'I still love you'. And if it was her ears, she wasn't sure if they'd come from her lips, or Chase's.

~*~*~*~*~

This time when Jenna woke, it was to the russet glow of sunset filtering through the curtains and the smell of pine and meadow grasses, as they released the heat of the day. A gentle breeze cooled the room and the steady thud of Chase's heart beating beneath her ear echoed the flow of blood in her own sated body.

Now she was draped over him, and his arms and legs held her close. Even the sight of their clothes, scattered where they'd fallen in their earlier haste, filled her with a feeling of contentment. Jenna wanted it to last forever.

There had to be a way they could put the past behind them and start again. After all that had transpired over the last couple of days, surely Chase was feeling the same things she was. Wasn't he?

As he began to stir, Chase absently brushed his knuckles up and down her spine and rubbed his two day old whiskers against her cap of curls. Something about the innocence of his actions crumbled another of her heart's defenses.

Looking up at his handsome face Jenna realized this Chase wasn't the same boy she'd fallen in love with as a naïve girl. He wasn't the same reckless youth she feared for every time he'd driven, or ridden behind, one of those damn chuckwagons.

The person holding her close now was a man who'd paid the price for that recklessness, one who'd struggled back and matured into a far better version of himself.

Someone she could trust to never leave her the way her parents had.

The light bounced off the mirror hanging on the back of the door, driving her hidden fears from the shadows. Deep down she knew blaming them for dying was irrational but still couldn't help feeling abandoned.

Was that why she hadn't fought back that day at the hospital? Is that why she'd given up so easily and walked away, leaving her with a gaping hole inside to this day?

Jenna threw open the door she'd kept locked in the back of her mind since the day they died as the last rays of the sun breached the split in the curtains. A chill inched up her back and she sucked her bottom lip between her teeth.

No. That wasn't right. She had to stop deluding herself. Truth was, she'd lived with that hole until two days ago when Chase stepped back into her life and filled it.

His arms tightened around her and rubbed the back of her leg with his foot. "God, Jen. It feels so good to hold you again."

The warmth in his voice filled her heart to overflowing. He *did* feel the same way!

Jenna lifted her head, about to tell him how she felt when her stomach protested its empty state with enough gusto to make a hungry trucker proud.

Chase laughed and bent his head, kissing her deeply and stirring a different kind of hunger. At another growl from her mid-section, he broke away and chuckled. "Guess I'll have to fill that hole huh?"

Hearing her thoughts echoed stunned her, but Chase didn't seem to notice as he tossed her off to the side and gave her bottom a playful swat then reached for his crumpled jeans. "Besides, what would I hold on to next time if I let that sexy little butt of yours wither away to nothing?"

She didn't find her voice till his hand was on the doorknob. "Next time?"

Chase looked back over his shoulder and winked, his gaze laced with a hint of that possessive heat it had earlier. "Yah. Next time."

The door clicked shut behind him, and Jenna grabbed his pillow and buried her face in it to muffle the giddy squeal she couldn't stifle if she wanted to.

Chase whistled as he made Jenna's sandwich. Like him, she loved her mustard.

The little devil on his left shoulder poked him; maybe if he slathered it on really thick, it would drip off the corner of her mouth and he could lick it off for her.

The angel on his right snapped to and produced the memory of his jealous outburst after she'd called him Bart and his tune faltered. He'd known at the time he was being ridiculous, but it hadn't stopped him. He'd had an overwhelming need to have Jenna acknowledge *him.* The angel pricked him again. Okay, okay, he'd had an overwhelming need for her to be *his* again.

The pipes behind the wall banged as Jenna turned on the shower and the devil reached around from behind and knocked the angel off.

Chase's mind filled with thoughts of Jenna rubbing soap on her breasts and tweaking her nipples as her eyes glazed over. He pictured her lips parting slightly and her hand reaching between her legs. Her slender thighs squeezing together and her fingers slick with soap stimulating her—

"I hope you know what the hell you're doing."

His eyes popped open and the little devil did a jig in celebration of how fast Chase's body came to attention. Thank God his back was turned. "Umm, making sandwiches?"

Wooden feet scrapped the floor behind him as JT spun one of the chairs at the island around and flopped down on it. "Don't be a smart ass."

The jingle of keys hit the counter top and Chase winced. Uh oh, he'd completely forgotten about Jenna's car.

Little red bugger with the pitch fork puffed out his chest and grinned - yup, but so did she. Chase shook his head and focused on cutting the bread. "Did you have trouble getting it out?"

"No, no, nothing to it."

The keys started to rattle and Chase finished cutting through the sandwiches a little more forcefully than necessary. He knew that tone.

"Nothing, unless you count having to crawl around in the mud only to discover somewhere to hook a tow line must've been an option on those cars. Or, the fact that, after six attempts to pull it loose didn't work, I had to traipse up a forty-five degree incline to find a tree trunk big enough to tie the winch cable to." JT's boots started to thump against the chairs foot rails.

Chase stuck his head in the fridge to put the sandwich fixings away and had the sudden urge to slam the door on himself.

"Course, once it was finally out, there was nothing to driving back and saddling up a horse so I could ride all the way up there to drive Jenna's car back. All so I could turn around and saddle a second horse so I could head out again to round up the first one. Because believe it or not, as good as I am...EVEN I CAN'T PULL OFF DRIVING TWO VEHICLES AT ONCE!"

The chicken-shit guy with the pitchfork went 'poof' and the sound of the fridge door closing echoed through the kitchen.

Then again, looking at JT's face, maybe the little creep with the horns had the right idea.

Chase set the plates off to the side and scrubbed his hands through his hair. Anger he could handle; disappointment, not so much. "JT, listen—"

JT shot off his chair as though stuck with a cattle prod. "No, you listen." His gnarled finger poked the air close to the end of Chase's nose. "Having to pluck Jenna's car out by myself ain't what's got my goat, boy. It's *why* I had to pluck it out all by my lonesome that's got my dander up."

Chase own temper sparked and he narrowed his eyes. Pissed about the car, okay, but sticking his nose into Chase's personal life wasn't. "You got something to say, say it."

JT braced his hands on the counter and leaned close. "You know damn well what I'm talking about. You think I'm stupid? I know how you spent your afternoon. Why do you think I rescued Jenna's car on my own?"

"You don't know a damn thing."

It was JT's turn to narrow his eyes. "Oh really. So you running around barefoot and...," he glanced at Chase's baby smooth chest and missed a beat, "bald-chested...with the top button on your pants flapping in the breeze is how you usually run around. That it?"

The other little guy, the one with the halo, reappeared and cranked the heat up in Chase's cheeks. Okay, there was that. But it didn't mean he'd stand for JT pushing his nose in where it didn't belong. "Look, I appreciate what you did getting her car out and I'm sorry I wasn't there to help, but my personal life is just that; personal and none of your damn business. So let's drop it."

Hurt flashed across JT's face and the man seemed to deflate before Chase's eyes. "I see." He turned and headed for the door then paused with his hand on the knob. "Get mad at me if you want, but I'm gonna say my piece. You best be thinking with the head on your shoulders because I've known that little girl almost as long as I've known you and would hate to think you're just playing with her affections."

He couldn't have hit harder had he used his fist. Chase grabbed the edge of the counter and hung his head to regain his bearings. Playing with her affections? Did JT really think he was that much of an asshole?

"And you might want to call Jared back." The door banged shut and the porch boards bounced under his boots as JT stormed off. "Preferably before she gets out of the shower, if you know what's good for you."

Chase lifted his head and stared at the door. What the hell did that mean? Marching into the den across the way he grabbed the phone and dialed Jared's number. JT was being an idiot. He wasn't playing with Jenna's affections. Was he? As he listened to the ring on the other end, his mind turned over everything that transpired since he and Jenna ran into each other again.

They weren't the same people they'd been four years ago, but her smile, her laugh, her fiery response to his touch and the way she felt cuddled up to him; those things hadn't changed. Until now he hadn't realized how much he'd missed them - and wanted them back.

"Hello, Jared here."

Chase's mind snapped back to the present. "Hey Jared, its Chase. You left a message to call?"

"Chase, yah, sure did. Thanks for getting back to me. Listen, I'm kind of in a bind and need to ask a huge favor."

They'd come up in the rodeo ranks together and Jared had stood by Chase's family more often than he could count; there wasn't much he wouldn't do for the man in return. "Shoot."

"You know Tory's due anytime right?"

Chase swallowed, propped his hip on the desk and banished the worry from his voice before answering. Jared's wife had miscarried twice before. "Everything okay?"

"Oh, yah, everything's great. In fact, they're going to induce her this Friday."

Chase's heart swelled for his buddy. "That's wonderful...wait a minute, this Friday?" How could Jared drive his team if he was at the hospital with his wife? "But that's opening day?"

"Sure is; which is why I'm calling. We're hoping you'll drive in my place."

"Drive?" Chase's hand squeezed the receiver

and his heart rate picked up. Then the other shoe dropped pushing sweat out his pores. If he didn't do this, Jared's rig would be out of the Rangeland Derby and any chance Chase had of sharing in the winning purse would be over.

Could he do it, though? Could he pick up the lines and run a team around that track again?

"Chase, I know what I'm asking. But you've been instrumental in training these horses. They're familiar with you, and frankly, I don't trust anyone else to do it. So, what do you say?"

It was true. He'd worked with them for over a year and knew everything there was to know about Jared's team. Chase pinched the bridge of his nose. What choice was there? He had to try for the money. Without it, the ranch was lost and so was canvas sponsorship money Jared relied on to keep his team running.

A tingle of excitement shot down his legs bringing him back to his feet. This could be the chance to prove he could still do it and maybe finally put the ghost of his accident to rest. The mere thought of it eased a fraction of the tension from the brittle muscles in Chase's shoulders.

Rolling them in their sockets at the unfamiliar feel, he stared at his reflection in the window and faced a hard truth. Part of him wanted to do this, but an even bigger part needed to.

"Chase? You there?"

"Yah, I'm here. And of course I'll drive the Stampede for you." The 'yeehaw' on the other end brought a smile to Chase's face. "Besides, if I didn't, I'm not sure what Tory'd kick my sorry ass harder for, the loss of your sponsorship money when you're about to have another mouth to feed, or you off driving when that little mouth arrives."

Movement out the corner of his eye caught his attention. Jenna stood in the doorway not moving, her face was the colour of wall-paper paste, and whatever Jared said next was lost on Chase.

"I'll have to call you back buddy." Without looking away from her, Chase slid his thumb over the disconnect button. "Jen? You okay?"

She rubbed her hands on her legs and her eyes darted around the room as though looking for an escape. "So, Jared huh?"

"Yah, that was Jared." Why was she looking like he committed some crime?

"As in, Chuckwagon owner, Jared Kinnley."

Chase had a feeling he was about to walk into a mine-field he couldn't hope to clear but didn't have a clue how to avoid it. "Yes, but I don't see why my talking to him has you so upset."

Now *she* seemed bewildered. "But, the modeling...I thought you'd...."

"Jen what are you talk—"

"...given it up—"

At a loss as to what was going on, Chase threw his hands in the air. "You thought I gave up modeling? Honey, you're not making any sense."

Her lip started to tremble and her voice cracked on her answer. "No! Racing, damn it."

"Quit Racing?" Where did she get that idea? Understanding slammed home and the lights came on for Chase. Of course it hadn't, everything happened so fast the subject hadn't come up, there'd been no time for it to.

He was working off ranch with the modeling thing, so why *wouldn't* she believe he was done with racing? Until a few weeks ago, he had been.

The growing knot in his stomach turned to ice. "That's what you thought?"

She nodded her head without speaking. Chase wanted to run and bar the door but was afraid if he moved she'd bolt. Somehow he had to make her understand. "Jen, wait. If you'll let me explain—"

Her voice sounded flat and she started to turn away. "Explain what? That you're driving again?

No need to, I got that."

Giving in to his rising panic he reached for her but she flinched away and his arm dropped to his side like a broken tree branch.

Who was he kidding? They were in exactly the same place they'd been four years ago and until the ranch was secure there was nothing he could do about it.

Chase took a step forward. She took one back, tearing a chunk out of his heart and creating a gaping chasm between them. Any fledgling hopes he'd begun to harbor crumbled before his eyes. "I don't know what to say."

Jenna cradled her arms around herself and with a sad smile shifted her foot toward the hallway. "Hey it was fun while it lasted, right?"

Before Chase could say anything, she stood taller and raised her hand. "Don't bother showing me to the door, I know my way out."

He hated letting her go like this. "Jen wait."

"Good bye Chase."

He stared at the empty spot where she'd been and listened to the front door close, unable to bring himself to try and stop her again.

Chase balled his hands into fists and gritted his teeth, wanting to hit something and ease the dull ache throbbing in his extremities as the engine in her little beater sputtered to life.

He didn't move until her tail lights winked out behind the trees and vanished into the night, and then, only to give into his impulse to hit something.

Howling, Chase hung his head and banged his fists on the window frame.

Chapter 9

"Tamra! Get in here."

Marla's fingers were frozen over her keyboard and a mile wide grin split her artfully done up face. These were even better than she'd hoped.

"You bellowed, oh wise one?"

She glanced up and shot a frown at her assistant. "I'm in too good a mood right now, so I'll let that pass."

Tamra smirked. "Wow, I stand suitably chagrined."

Marla's grin snuck back over her face. Kid had gumption, had to give her that. "Has Ms. Cordell been paid for these?"

A quizzical look bordering on annoyance skidded over Tamra's face. "Of course, why?"

"And she signed the waiver relinquishing rights?"

Tamra perched her hip on the corner of Marla's desk and crossed her arms over her tablet, hugging it to her chest. "Yes, as always."

Marla rubbed her hands together then spun her computer screen toward Tamra. "Excellent. Now take a look at these." A wave of satisfaction at the stunned look on her prickly little assistant's face rolled over her.

"Oh my god, these are incredible." Her tablet slid to the desktop and she crouched down hitting the scroll button on the mouse. "He's fabulous."

"Ain't he just." Marla tapped Tamra's wrist to gain back control of the mouse and clicked on one specific shot. "And this, my dear, is what I want you to overlay onto the 'Wild' template and send off to Trisha immediately."

Tamra's eyes widened as she took in the picture before her, then she slowly lifted her head to stare Marla in the eye. "But don't we have a non recognition clause with him? You can see his face in this one."

Marla reached out and patted her cheeks. "No, actually you can see his profile in three quarter. The clause in his contract states we can't use his complete face."

Tamra's jaw dropped. "Oh wow. You really are good - devious, but good."

"A well played trick of the trade, my young apprentice."

"He's not going to be happy about this, you know that right?"

Marla spun the screen back and shrugged. "Lesson Number Two: Never ask permission when you can hand them a big fat cheque and automatically be forgiven.

Even our darling Mr. Donavan will have a big smile on his handsome face when he sees how much money he's going to make.

Besides, he won't know anything about it until it's too late."

"Save a horse, ride a cowboy! Yahoo! How 'bout it, darlin'?"

Jenna ducked her head and hurried past a football field sized tent located at the north end of the grounds. Cowboy's annual home for the ten days of Stampede, complete with drunken patrons and the occasional old-fashion brawl spilling out everywhere at all hours of the day or night, always made her nervous.

It was one thing to go to the famous hangout's brick and mortar location with Tina. This was something else entirely.

Kate on the other hand wasn't so inhibited and raised her voice over the pounding music. "You're a bit wet behind the ears for my taste sweetie, but thanks anyway."

143

Jenna grabbed her aunt's sleeve and tugged her past the revelers. "Don't encourage the inebriated tourist Auntie. You don't know where he's been or if he's had his shots lately."

Kate's giggle sounded much younger than her age. "Oh I think he's had more than his share of shots lately. Besides, I'm just having a little fun with the boy, that's all."

The smell of stale beer and spilled drinks receded as they rounded the corner toward the back entrance of the BMO Centre. The spacious, well appointed convention facility was used for everything from auto and truck shows to entertaining William and Kate. It was also home to the Stampede's art show, and where Jenna had to get set up in time for opening tomorrow.

On the Thursday of every year, several pieces were auctioned off, leaving room for mid-week exhibitors like her to move in for the final few days of the show. Only hitch was you couldn't move in during open hours and the show didn't close until around midnight every night.

Fits of crying and a lack of sleep since she'd left Chase at the Flying D had eroded Jenna's enthusiasm and her feet felt like they were full of lead.

Still, when she and Auntie Kate got to the bay door, she managed to dredge up a smile seeing her friends waiting there to help her load everything in.

Mr. Deagle had been kind enough to offer both his trailer and body, bringing Mrs. G. along for the ride and Kate had asked Pattie to throw her services in too. But it still felt like a daunting task ahead of them.

Mr. Deagle stepped up and rallied the troupes. "What say we get this show on the road, shall we? I've got a bag of them mini donuts in the truck just dying to be eaten." He winked at Mrs. Goreman as he rolled open the overhead door and she blushed. "Might even share a few if you play your cards right."

Kate flung her arm around Mrs. G.'s shoulder and laughed. "Any man willing to share those sugar coated cinnamon temptations is a keeper."

Jenna swiped at the burning sensation firing up under her eyelids for the thousandth time in the last week. Chase had always shared them. He'd even made a special trip into the city just to bring a bag back for her the year she'd sprained an ankle and couldn't come.

In spite of telling herself she had to stop thinking about him, she'd driven herself crazy each night he'd raced, praying he'd made it through safely and knew he was in a top spot going into the finals.

And as if that wasn't enough, she'd been haunted by the image burned into her brain of him and the mustang. The unmistakable resemblance to her work compelled her to pull the tarp off and finish his statue, in the hopes of exorcising him from her system. It hadn't worked.

"Honey, which booth is yours?"

Kate's voice broke in and Jenna snapped to attention and kicked her wishy-washy determination back in line.

There were still three days to go till the end of the Greatest Outdoor Show on Earth for another year, and until then there was nothing she could do about her unresolved feelings for Chase. It was time to focus on her career and this show.

Kate had busted her butt, and if Jenna didn't want to let either her Aunt or herself down now, she'd better get with the program. "It's in the center on the far side of the wine bar, third from the left."

Pattie chimed in and whipped an imaginary lasso in the air above her head. "All right, get along little doggies. Let's move 'em on out."

As everyone got to work, the fireworks show lit

up, signaling the end of the grandstand performance that followed the chuckwagon races each night, and Jenna's hard won game-face slipped.

Sending Kate after the others with assurances she was right behind her, Jenna pulled out her phone and looked up the race results on the internet only to have her worse fear confront her.

Each night, the top four teams raced last and tonight there'd been a wagon wreck in the final heat.

Chase was in that top four.

It hadn't been him, but that hadn't stopped the nightmares and the next morning on her way in, walking through the adjacent hall where the slice, dice and julienne hawkers were getting set to open, Jenna wished she had earplugs.

Everyone was buzzing about the accident. Snippets of 'thank goodness it wasn't worse' and 'at least the horses were okay' beat at her from all sides.

Of course the horses were important. Everyone knew they were part of each team owner's family but what about the driver? Why was it people forgot there were men on that track too?

Because not everyone is as close to it as you are.

Jenna leaned against the wall at the entrance to the art show area and tried to put things into perspective. No, not everyone was as close to it as she was. Most of the people in the stands were from the city or were tourists who came for the thrill and spectacle of the sport. To them it was just a show.

A show she hated.

Jenna took a deep breath and purposefully changed her focus to the boulder ringed indoor fountains and ponds framing the pathways inside the Western Oasis. The fiber-optic waterfall behind the wine bar was alive with waves of aqua and purple, a backdrop visible from every angle of the room and the special mood lighting orchestrating the serene feel the show got its name for soothed her frayed nerves.

Beautifully appointed booths or salons, as they were referred to, ran the perimeter of the massive space with an inner ring of the same converging on the wine bar in the center of the room. Paintings, sculptures and multimedia works of every description were displayed within. Some even life size like Marty, or bigger. The thought of her bronze nemesis made her smile.

This was her world. The one she chose because she could get lost in its beauty. Art had become a balm for her soul and her heart's joy after breaking up with Chase. Relocating to the coast and taking her art degree at the Vancouver School of Fine Art had been a big part of putting the horror of Chase's accident and their shattered dreams behind her so she could get on with her life.

Spellbound, Jenna slowly moved her feet forward, heading toward her salon, taking note of the who's who of the western art world around her. Andrew Kiss, Jody Skinner, Sam Terakedis and dozens more all represented in this one place. The shock of being a participant rather than a spectator was starting to sink in.

A world with people like Doug Levitt who'd done the 2008 record breaking Stampede poster, entitled 'A Man of His People' a near life size painting of a native chief in full regalia on horseback. And his salon partner, Ken Mayernik, a 3-D bronze sculptor she'd admired for years; a man who could turn a modern rancher on a quad into a collector's piece of western heritage. Name after name of people she'd studied to hone her craft were everywhere.

Now, her work was being showcased in the same room. A chill settled over Jenna that had nothing to do with the air-conditioning.

This was what she'd strived so hard for and what she needed to focus on, not the ashes of the past, no matter how hot the fire had burned. Pulling her jacket from her shoulders and sticking it in the draped off 'back room' in her section, Jenna admitted it was time to grow up.

When the final race on Sunday was over, she'd have to face Chase. She'd have to tell him their brief reunion, as bittersweet as it was, had been a mistake. That she couldn't be a part of his world and still be able to create in hers. Neither her heart nor her art would survive. It was the least she could do after leaving like she did the other day. They both needed closure to move on.

The organ in question protested and squeezed in her chest until she had to sit down. *Why couldn't he give up racing? Why couldn't he love her enough; they could've been so happy.*

"Good morning."

A cheerful voice behind her stopped the threatening tears and Jenna shoved her failed dreams back into their dark corner. She blinked rapidly before turning around and when she did, a friendly smile in a kind face, greeted her. "Oh. Hello. I mean good morning." Sheesh, that sounded intelligent.

She must've groaned out loud because his smile widened and he stuck out his hand. "Hi. I take it, you're Jenna?"

"Yes, I am." Her hand vanished into his as she returned his shake.

"Thought I'd take a moment to introduce myself and welcome you to the merry mad house that is our little show here. A myriad of twelve hour days, overpriced junk food, aching feet and a group of the best folks you'd ever hope to meet. Hi, my name's Doug."

Jenna's eyes popped. She knew of only one Doug in the show. "Doug Levitt?"

He grinned and a bit of pink rose in his cheeks. "Yah, but don't tell anyone, okay?"

His genuine smile helped and Jenna began to relax. Until she tried to come up with a topic they could break the ice on, and she channeled her inner fan-girl instead. "Okay, but only if you tell me where you get your inspiration. Your work is so varied and you're so prolific, I can't imagine where you get it all from."

Jenna wanted to bite her tongue out but he just

smiled wider. Either he was too much of a gentleman to add to her embarrassment, or he didn't mind her less than stellar opener.

Gesturing to the chair she'd vacated, Doug held it out for her, then, pulled the other one out from behind her make-shift desk for himself.

"A lot of my ideas come from trying to imagine what it must've been like for the native people when they encountered the settlers for the first time. And because I'm dedicated to my art telling as an authentic story as possible, I've done a lot of research, which in turn, has continued to fire my imagination. It's sort of a 'the more you know, the less you know', kind of thing."

Chase's mother was Nakota. Jenna choked that line of thought off with a shift of her shoulders. "You said 'a lot' come that way. What else have you found works for you?"

He leaned his head back and stroked his chin, giving her a penetrating look. "You do realize, if I tell you, I might have to kill you."

Jenna wasn't sure if she should laugh or not, then Doug winked and waved his hand at her.

"Nah, just kidding. One of the best ways I've found is The Artist's Ride every August in Wyoming."

"Artist's ride? I don't think I'm familiar with it?"

"That's not so unusual. See, the local First Nation's people do reenactments in period costume, both with and without horses, and the artists take photos to use as fodder for their work. So even as an artist, unless you're really deep into the authentic western work, it might not have come up on your radar."

"Wow it sounds amazing. Do you go every year?"

"I wish. Unfortunately, as I'm sure you know, the life of an artist isn't one that allows for a lot of expenditures so, no, I have to limit myself to once every so often, what with the travel involved and cost of the ride itself."

Jenna frowned at the wistful tone in his voice. "Isn't there anything closer you could do?"

He shook his head. "No, there's nothing like it in Canada."

Just then a woman in an expensive looking western outfit, complete with a full-length leather skirt and turquoise jewelry dripping everywhere, entered Jenna's booth. Doug glanced at her and gave Jenna a thumbs-up as he stood to leave and mouthed. "This one's a buyer. Good luck."

Boy he wasn't kidding. By the time the woman was through she'd purchased three of Jenna's larger pieces and two other buyers, having noticed her interest, relieved her of five of the mid sized ones.

Jenna was ecstatic. Seven of her twenty-five were sold already and it wasn't even lunch time on the first day. At this rate she'd need to bring in more or risk running out before the show was over.

A streak of color that was her Auntie Kate popped around the corner and she squealed when she saw the red 'sold' dots already scattered throughout Jenna's booth. "Hot damn! How many have you sold?"

Kate's excitement contagious, it was all Jenna could do not to squeal too, the butterflies in her stomach were so strong. "Seven. Can you believe it?"

"And you thought you weren't ready." Her aunt smirked and crossed her arms. "And now I get to indulge my inner brat and say I told you so. Ready? Here it comes. I told you so."

The laughter in her voice and twinkle in her eye took any sting out of her words. "Okay, you earned it and I can't thank you enough for going behind my back. So go ahead, gloat away at my expense."

Kate's penciled on brows shot toward her now

purple tipped hairline "Behind your back?" Then she tapped her chin and conceded. "Okay, guess I did, but that's not the point."

Jenna wrapped arms around Kate. "No, it isn't, and I really do want to thank you."

"Oh honey, I'm so glad it's working out so well." She leaned her head back and looked at Jenna, and her voice softened further. "Now, when were you planning on telling me what's going on with you and Chase Donavan?"

Jenna momentarily reverted to the seventeen year old she'd been when her aunt asked a similar question after she lost her virginity to Chase on prom night. "How do you know about that?" Then she smacked herself in the head at the smug look on Kate's face. *Great, until you opened your big mouth she hadn't.*

Kate reached out and grabbed the hand Jenna had abused her forehead with. "I heard a rumor, one that by your reaction is apparently true." With a gentle nudge Jenna found herself back in her chair. "Want to tell me what's up."

Jenna took a deep breath, and sat up. "Nothing."

Her aunt's eyebrow shot higher this time, but she didn't say anything, just stared at her. Jenna knew that look. It meant Kate wasn't budging till Jenna spit it out. "Okay, we bumped into each other...over a job actually...and things got a little intense at one point." Damn it. A lump was forming in her throat. "Anyway, he's still racing...so I realize it was...a mistake...for both of us...and—"

"You sure about that?"

Had she just said what she thought she did? She must have, because Kate's face at that moment carried the most serious expression Jenna had ever seen on it, and it scared her a bit. "Auntie?"

"I'm going to tell you something and I don't want you to interrupt me until I'm done, okay?"

Jenna gulped. "Okay?"

"Before you came to me, I was madly in love with a stunt man I'd met at the Ranchman's one night." Her eyes seemed to focus in that far off past. "He was the most handsome, charming, wonderful man I'd ever met. And boy did we have a time. That was the best summer of my entire life." She closed her eyes. "Then that fall, he proposed making me the happiest woman alive...the next day one of the other stunt men was killed on set.

"I suddenly saw a different future from the one I'd had the night before." Kate reopened her eyes, and the regret and loss filling their depths struck

Jenna straight through the heart. "I gave him his ring back."

"Oh Auntie, I never knew."

Kate sighed. "But that's not the end of it. He tried for six months to change my mind, to give us a second chance. I refused. Then a couple of years after you came to be with me, I ran into his sister. You know what she told me?"

"What?"

"That he'd quit the stunt world right after I gave his ring back, and that he was too hurt and proud to tell me. He wanted me to love him in spite of his job." Kate snorted. "He married his assistant that same year and now has five grandkids."

A moment from the past popped into Jenna's head. Kate had tucked her in, but she'd had a nightmare and sought her out in her room, only to find her aunt huddled on her bed in a ball with silent tears leaking down her face. Jenna had crawled in beside her and snuggled up to her back. "That night I came in your room—"

"Yes, that was the day I found out what we'd thrown away over a misunderstanding based in fear and our stubborn youthful pride. I've never loved another since. Not sure I ever will, all because I was too afraid to give us that second chance."

"As much as I see the similarity, in my case it's different. Chase won't give up racing—"

"Shh, I'm not finished." Kate straightened her spine; her usual vitality leaking back into her posture. "Last night, I was over at the Nashville North tent waiting for Pattie and I met the most interesting fellow. He got to talking about the plight of ranchers these days, and how hard it is to keep the operations afloat.

"He also told me about one of the driver's in this year's Rangeland who's like a son to him, and how he's out there trying to win the money to save his ranch before the bank can take it from him. Want to know what my new friend's name is?"

The hair on Jenna's arms had been rising with every word and now stood on end. Her voice came out a whisper. "What?"

"JT."

Chapter 10

Late Sunday afternoon Chase found himself at the far side of the wine bar for the third time since Jenna had set up her booth. After the near miss he'd had Thursday night with the other driver losing control of his team and damn near crashing into Chase's, he'd felt an overwhelming need to see her.

But each time he came in, she'd been busy with a customer, just like she was now, so he'd plunked himself down on one of the tall stools on the far side of the wine bar then when she was free - he'd chicken out.

He was an idiot.

Absently swirling the straw in his Pepsi, he watched her put a red dot on the big sculpture in the center of her booth and roll it behind the curtain at the back. Seeing all the red dots she had in there did his heart good. He'd always known she was talented and had badgered her for ages to go to art school. The success she was having at this show was proof he'd been right.

The customer left the booth and Chase smiled as he watched her break into what she'd call her 'Snoopy dance'. Her denim vest and jeans hugged her curves and his eyes traveled the length of her wiggling form of their own accord. He took a pull on his drink to ease his suddenly dry mouth.

Damn she looked good enough to eat. But that wasn't why his heart rate had picked up and an ant hill had moved into his belly.

Watching her in her element and thinking about what it had been like over the last four years on his own made him admit his true feelings. He wanted more than just her body; he wanted all of her, body, mind and soul. She was his and nothing would be right in his life without her.

Chase sat up straight in his chair and planted his hat back on his head. After tonight was over, he was through with racing. Money or no money, what good was fighting for the ranch with no one to share it with and no one to pass it on to?

The world seemed to brighten before his eyes and Chase felt the first real smile hit his face in over a week. By God, he loved her and he was going to get her back.

"Whoa there, cowboy. You'd better be careful where you aim that weapon. A smile like that could do a lady's resistance a lot of damage."

Chase turned to find a beautiful dark haired woman with bright blue eyes giving him the once over. Looking past her to Jenna he tipped his hat without looking back. "Sorry ma'am, but this cowboy's already branded."

She glanced over her shoulder then back at him. "Lucky girl."

He tore his gaze from Jenna and winked at his companion. "Nope, lucky boy." At least he hoped he'd be around nine o'clock tonight. She gave him a genuine smile and he hopped off his bar stool. "If you'll excuse me I—"

A blast over the loud speakers drowned out the rest of Chase's words and a niggling feeling crept over him as he listened to the voice. He was sure he'd heard it before.

"If I could have your attention please, we're about to reveal the winner of the 'Wild' campaign contest sponsored by the world renowned Evian Cologne for Men. As you know the search for the perfect representative for this new and exciting cologne has been extensive, but at long last I'm happy to say we've found the perfect face."

The woman with the dark hair placed her hand on his arm. "I should've introduced myself, Chase, my name's Trisha and I was one of the judges for this. If we hurry we can catch the reveal on the monitor over there."

Chase's mind zeroed in on one thing. Had she said face? The sounds in the room receded into a tunnel and he gave her no resistance as she tugged him toward the screen. A sinking feeling in his gut, Chase sought out Jenna and the next several seconds played out in horrible slow motion.

The sold sculpture in the middle of her booth had been removed and she was rolling another in to take its place.

Trisha squeezed his arm and he turned his head to see Marla flipping back a satiny cover to reveal a huge poster. A similar motion drew his attention back to Jenna as she pulled the cover off the new piece.

She glanced up at the monitor then spun back to the unveiled sculpture. Her head came up and in spite of his internal alarms going off, Chase couldn't look away.

Her eyes, the size of saucers found his and a deafening buzz flooded his ears as the expression on her chalk-white face tore into him.

Guilt.

He wasn't seeing things. It really was him up

on the screen in the poster, and in the center of Jenna's booth as a sculpture.

In both places his arms were reaching up to encircle a horse's neck and its mane was merged with his hair as it fell down his bare back. The animal's face was over his shoulder on the one side - and his was turned so you could see it on the other.

His world tipped. In both places you could clearly see his face.

Everything clicked in that moment and anger stirred the bile in his stomach. Son of a bitch! His contract was clear, his face wasn't to be used, but Marla's actions were nothing compared to Jenna's betrayal. His face out there would, without a doubt, cause him a passel of humiliation, but seeing something he'd considered so special and private, something he'd been so happy to share with her alone, was what was ripping his heart out.

Heat raced up his neck and the back of his head started to hurt as the muscles in his extremities twitched under his rising temper. No wonder she hadn't tried to see him after that day at the ranch.

She'd never intended to. The center of his chest felt like he'd been kicked by a bull.

She knew how important keeping this whole

stupid thing secret was to him and she hadn't given a damn.

She'd gotten what she needed for her precious art and made money on his picture to boot sullying the memory of what had happened between them that day.

Did she hate him that much? Was this her way of getting back at him?

"Oh my god, it's him! Right there, the *'Wild'* guy is right here!"

Through the red haze and hurt, Chase felt Trisha lean against him and give a push. "You might want to make a run for it, stud."

One look at the feminine wave headed toward him and Chase didn't need to be told twice. He'd deal with Marla...and Jenna later. Right now he needed to get the hell out of Dodge or get trampled.

Bolting in the opposite direction from his new admirers Chase tipped his hat further down over his face and hit the door at a run. He didn't stop until he was out on the midway where he was sure to blend in with the crowds and gain a moment to think.

Planting his butt against a guard rail he leaned his head back to catch his breath only to have it turn into a snarl. His face was being broadcast throughout the Stampede grounds on multiple

Jumbotron screens everywhere. He could even hear the echo of the announcement from the far side of the grandstand where it faced the infield. The same infield his fellow ranchers and peers would all be watching from.

Jenna. Why?

Jenna pulled the covering off the piece Mr. Deagle and Mrs. G. had agreed to retrieve from her apartment this morning in case she sold the big one and gasped. It wasn't the one she'd meant. It was supposed to be the one with the deer coming down the waterfall, instead it was Chase's.

> *"...at long last I'm happy to say we've found the perfect face."*

Jenna's pulse slowed to a crawl as she looked at the monitor across the way, a sick feeling building inside. Marla stepped to the side of the screen and tossed the cover off the *'Wild'* poster sporting her picture of Chase and Thunderhead from their day on the ridge.

She looked down in horror; the same picture

that had inspired her to finish the piece at her feet - a piece that was never to be seen by anyone but her. And that wasn't the worst of it, somehow she must've given 'Models to Go' the wrong memory card.

The enormity of her mistake made her legs weak and acid creep up into her chest. She'd edited the pictures she meant to keep only for herself off the original card before turning them in to Marla but not the back-up copy. She must've delivered it instead.

An irresistible force lifted her chin and she came face to face with Chase. As she watched her betrayal harden his features, she felt the color bleed from hers.

Oh god, what had she done?

She'd decided to take a run at the second chance Kate hadn't, racing or no racing, and had been hard pressed to wait until after the finals tonight to seek Chase out. She'd been hoping he felt the same way, and would want to try again too. The look on his face now dashed all hope of that.

And it was all her fault!

"Oh my god, it's him! Right there, the *'Wild'* guy. Look!"

With one last scathing glance at her, Chase

pulled his hat down over a face black as thunder and darted toward the back exit; a sea of stampeding woman building in numbers behind him.

"And best of all ladies, the 'Wild' man himself should be getting ready as we speak to thrill us all in tonight's Rangeland Derby finals. You all know who he is by now so let's head over there and cheer him on!"

One thought blasted past everything else in Jenna's mind cutting her to the quick.

Oh God, Chase was driving tonight!

Barely aware her legs were moving she shot for the same exit Chase had vanished through moments ago.

She had to get to him and fix this before he got out on the track. In this state he'd never be able to concentrate on the race. This time he could really get himself killed!

Jenna rounded the corner of the BMO centre and spun around frantically trying to figure out which way he'd gone. Every avenue she looked at was a mass of people milling from one midway game or ride to another. The bells and whistles were deafening and the flashing lights around her disorienting, adding to her rising panic.

Heaven help her, he could be anywhere.

Well standing here like a ninny isn't going to help Jenna, so move. Pick a lane!

Diving headlong into the throng, Jenna pushed and jostled her way forward to a chorus of 'hey' and 'watch it' but she didn't care.

The smell of roasted turkey legs, barbequed beef and cotton candy assaulted her nose and hysterical screams and laughter battered her from all sides. Then the delicious smell of cinnamon donuts triggered a flood of tears that choked her.

Oh please, Chase. Where are you?

A blast of light above her head caught her attention. The huge screen above her head filled with the 'Wild' poster. Her eyes darted across the heads of the carnival goers; it was on every screen. The magical moment Chase had so generously shared with her; their moment, was on display for all to see.

Jenna's mind raced, muddled by the mayhem of the midway as she turned in a slow circle, an island in an ocean of people. Each face not the one she so desperately sought.

Finding the proverbial needle would be easier.

Just as she was about to give up, the ocean of bodies surging around her parted and she spotted him. He was leaning against the side of the haunted house looking up at the screen above, his face a blank mask.

He'd never looked better to her. "Chase!" She shouldered her way toward him, never taking her eyes off him, afraid to lose him in the crowd again. "Chase!"

He finally heard her and suddenly his blank mask turned to one of pain and disbelief.

"You are the last person I want to see right now."

Jenna recoiled at the edge of disgust in his voice. "Wait, please listen. It was a mistake, I didn't know—"

He pulled his arm away before she could get hold of him and sneered. "What didn't you know Jenna? That the day we spent on that ridge was - until now - one of the best moments of my life? Or was it that you didn't know I'd be pissed you turned it into a public spectacle?"

She tried again to reach for him and he jerked away from her touch like she'd burnt him. The tears were free-flowing now and her voice cracked. "I didn't do this on purpose. That day was special for me too—"

"Stop." Chase held his hand out but it was the defeat in his voice that kept her at bay. "Just stop." His shoulders slumped and he started to turn away. "I can't do this Jen. Not now."

The muscles in Jenna's throat clamped down on the lump lodged there, strangling her voice and by the time she fought past it, it was too late.

Chase was gone.

Chapter 11

"Hey Donavan, you still talking to us ugly some-bitches now that you're a big star?"

Chase's molars hurt from grinding them as he stormed past the fourth 'funny guy' in as many stalls.

"Careful now. Pretty-boy Chase there, he's a wild-man." Mitch Hanson the top ranked driver tonight collapsed against one of his outriders, laughing so hard the other guy had to hold him up.

Bastard.

"Yah. Ha ha, real funny. Save it for the track smart guy." Another round of belly laughs echoed behind Chase as he escaped to where his team was being harnessed and relative safety.

Or so he thought.

"Lord almighty, boy. What the hell were you thinking?" JT wasn't having much luck keeping the smirk off his face. "What the hell possessed you to become a pansy-assed pinup boy?"

Chase's two outriders tipped their own faces down and wisely kept their mouths shut as they led the wagon team out toward the staging area. Good thing. He couldn't win if he hurt one of them bad enough they couldn't ride tonight.

JT however, was another story and Chase had had it. As soon as the wagon was clear, he tore his hat off his head, threw it to the ground and shouted through his teeth. "To save the fucking ranch! That's why."

JT jolted back and Chase's voice bounced back at him from the empty stall, echoing in the aftermath of his outburst. "I thought you of all people would understand that."

JT's crumpled face withered the anger in Chase, leaving behind - nothing.

"Why didn't you tell me, boy?"

He bent to retrieve his hat with a sigh. "Because my face was never supposed to be seen, and wouldn't have if it weren't for Jenna-Lynn."

JT stood silent for several heartbeats, then scratched his chin and squinted at Chase. "Jenna-Lynn now is it? What happened to Jenna?"

Bitterness welled at the sound of her name. "She used me, JT. This whole thing was all about furthering her career. The proof is sitting in the middle of her booth right now."

JT's face fell. "What? Our Jen? Why?"

"First call for the final heat. Driver's to the paddock."

Chase wished he knew why, but he didn't have time to think about it right now.

Setting his jaw, he drew the anger back to the surface, and smothered his bleeding heart. "You'll have to ask her JT, because I sure as hell won't."

He'd had enough wallowing. It wasn't only *his* future that was at stake. He had a race to win, and a ranch to save, even if he was the last Donavan to hold it and his only company was JT.

"Final call for heat ten. All wagons to the post."

"Gotta go." After switching his hat for the safety helmet hanging by the door, Chase headed out after his team, his parting shot sounding hollow even in his ears. "Wish me luck."

Chase didn't wait to hear if he did or not as he strode down the length of the barn trying to find his center and mentally prepare for the race.

It didn't matter how many times he'd climbed up into the seat to take the lines before a race, it still took all the nerve he could muster. Once the wagon was rolling he was fine, it was that first few moments that he had to get past every time.

As Chase walked up to his wagon he noticed

something was different. It took a moment for him to realize the big spot lights weren't trained on the infield like they usually were before a race. They were focused on the main stage instead. And he wasn't the only one thinking it was odd. Several of the men around him had puzzled looks on their faces.

"What's going on?"

Chase was relieved to see it was Cameron Carter who'd stepped up beside him and not one of the clowns he'd stormed by in the barns. Cameron was one of the few men he knew he could count on not to poke fun at him.

The man didn't like it when people made jokes at another's expense and Chase had seen many a hijinx fall under the heat of his steel-grey stare. Seemed not too many guys wanted to challenge a man over six feet tall that had been sending steers to the ground in record time for over a decade.

Chase nodded in greeting as he turned his attention back to the stage. "Not sure, but I guess we're about to find out."

A small parade of people marched up the ramp to the platform as the massive screens on either side of the infield blazed to life with the *'Wild'* man ad plastered all over them.

Chase groaned and tried to block it out by staring straight ahead. He attempted to run the race through his mind, but Marla's voice over the loudspeakers shot his concentration, drawing his attention back to her.

"Good evening everyone, and welcome to the final heat of the 2012 Rangeland Derby here on the hundredth anniversary of the Greatest Outdoor Show on Earth!" Her hands shot in the air and the crowd cheered.

Chase frowned.

As Marla waited for the stands to settle down, Trisha - he thought that was the name she'd said earlier - stepped up to the microphone.

"You see behind me the winner of the Evian *'Wild'* man cologne contest. And as one of the judges, it's my pleasure to let you know he's from right here in southern Alberta."

Another cheer rocked the stands and Chase pretended he didn't hear his outriders snicker.

"In fact, any minute now, he'll be coming out here on the track as one of the four finalists competing for the hundred-thousand dollar prize."

Chase snarled. He'd heard enough, but before he could launch himself up into the driver's seat, Cameron lifted his knee and planted his boot on the floor boards to block him.

"Chase I knew your brother and your father, good men both. But, as you know, they had a habit of barreling in without all the facts. You also know as well as I do how that turned out for them."

Chase saw the Track Marshall's signal for the first wagon to enter and start his warm up. "Cam, can't this wait till after the race?"

"Maybe, but in case you're in the mood to take after them and you get yourself in trouble out there because your head's up your ass, I think I'll say my piece now."

Chase didn't know if he should push the man aside or punch him in the mouth.

"Chase, I've known both you and Jenna-Lynn for a long time."

Chase pushed.

Cam pushed back and shot his other arm toward the screens. "Hold your horses damn it, and listen to me. I overheard you and JT and I'm here to tell you, I highly doubt she knew about *that* any sooner than you did."

"That life size replica of me in her booth says she did. Now, get the hell out of my way." Out of time and patience, Chase moved to shoulder past Cam and to gain the seat of his wagon.

Cam blocked again grabbing Chase's wrist as he reached for the lines. "Fine, but put this in your pipe and smoke it, ya knot-head. A friend of mine is considering buying that piece and asked if I'd give him my opinion. So I went and gave it the once over. So I happen to know, like most art, there's a date on that chunk of clay you're all pissed about; it's 2008. Four years ago."

Chase's outriders were shouting for him to get moving, but he grabbed Cam's shirt sleeve anyway. "What the hell does that have to do with anything?'

Cam grinned and glanced past Chase's shoulder. "You'll figure it out, but in the meantime hold on to this." His eyes narrowed and he seemed to focus on something or someone on stage. "You know that stuff about setting something free if you love it?"

"Yah."

"It's bullshit. I say when you find what you want you grab her by the ass and hold on. She makes it the full eight, you keep her. Simple as that." He nodded his head and winked. "Don't you have a race to run?"

"Chase! We're up, let's go!"

Cam clicked his tongue and smacked Chase's wheel horse on the rump. "Go on now, giddy-up."

177

Chase automatically compensated signaling for the lead horse to move with a flick of its line while taking up the slack controlling the one already in motion.

"Give 'em hell kid."

Chase nodded his hands too busy to do otherwise. "Thanks."

The crowd was chanting something he couldn't make out as Chase entered his warm-up and headed for the quarter-mark turning point, but that was fine. He didn't have to understand the words for the energy of so many people cheering and stamping their feet to get his adrenaline going. It was a rush unlike any other, and part of what kept this sport alive. It infected drivers, horses and fans alike, bringing them all back year after year.

Chase navigated the direction change back toward the infield smoothly then asked for a quick trot and the horses responded as one. The muscles under their sleek coats contracted and shifted in anticipation. They loved to run and were eager to get underway.

Coming into the barrels and lining his wheels up for his start position, Chase finally heard what the grandstand fans were cheering over the immediate noise of the infield around him and was sorry he had.

"Wild man! Wild man!"

The crowd, Cam's senseless words, Jenna's guilt-ridden face, and the jeers from the boys in the barn earlier, collided in his brain and Chase wished he had his own bit to chomp on. This was the last thing he needed.

"Donavan! You with us man?" Kyle Wilks, the outrider responsible for holding Chase's lead horses until the starting horn, brought him back into the game.

Chase shook the tension from his shoulders and tried to banish the crowd. "Yah, all good."

"Bull, but hey, if it helps, pretend they're chanting 'Donavan' instead of that shit."

Grateful for the man's reality check, Chase grinned and did exactly that. Until the Klaxon horn blew, and the announcer's famous call dominated the airwaves.

"Aannnnd they' rrrre off!"

Then there was no thought for anything but the twelve man, four wagon, twenty-four horse explosion of mayhem and the 'Half Mile of Hell' ahead.

~*~*~

Jenna charged into her booth at a dead run. "Auntie Kate! Where's Pattie?"

Kate managed to catch Jenna before she crashed into anything. "What the heck's going on, I show up and there's no one here...what? Pattie? Why do you want to know where she is?"

Struggling to catch her breath, Jenna did her best to tell her aunt what had happened in as short a time a possible. "So you see; I need her to help me get back into the barns and straighten this out before it's too late." A tear rolled from her eye and off the end of her nose, making Jenna sniff. "If he gets hurt again because of me, I'll never forgive myself."

Kate pursed her lips and pulled out her cell phone. "Pattie, how fast can you get me and Jenna back to the barns?"

Jenna leaned in so Pattie could hear her too. "Can you get hold of a golf cart or something?"

Kate closed her phone, dumped it in her skirt pocket and reached for Jenna's hand. "Already on her way with one. She'll meet us out front in five minutes, come on."

They hadn't taken two steps when Jenna's feet stopped. "Oh crap, the booth—"

A short dark haired figure materialized out of the muted pastel lighting of the wine bar across the way. "No worries, I'll hold down the fort while you're gone."

Recognition dawned and red crept into Jenna's vision. Tamra Eaton was one of the last people she wanted to see at the moment. "You have a lot of nerve showing your face around here after what you people did."

She rolled her eyes. "Yah, yah, whatever. Get to Chase now; beat me up later." She shooed her hands at them and a flash of guilt slipped out from under her mask, giving Jenna pause. "I got your back here already, now go."

"Jen come on, they're halfway through the ninth race. We have to hurry."

Jenna narrowed her eyes at Tamra. "All right and thank you; but fair warning, if anything happens to him, you and Marla will wish you'd never met me." Then she and Kate took off as fast as Kate's high-heeled boots would allow.

Jenna glanced back once and if she hadn't known better, she'd have sworn she caught a look of shame shadowing Tamra's face and her lips moving as though in silent prayer.

~*~*~

True to her word Pattie was out front with a golf cart a few minutes later and Jenna jumped on, dragging a gasping Kate behind her. "How fast can you get us to the wagons?"

A glint flashed in Pattie's eye. "Hold on to your hats, ladies." With no questions asked, she tromped her foot on the pedal and sent the cart careening out into the undulating masses of the midway. "Yeehaw!"

Jenna held on for dear life as Pattie threaded the cart through the crowds, more often than not sending people diving out of her way as she yelled. "Excuse me. Pardon me. Coming through." But it seemed to take forever.

The crowd from the grandstand could be heard cheering the winner of the ninth heat and Jenna's stomach kicked her ribs. "Hurry Pattie."

"We're almost there, hang on."

With that she cranked the wheel hard shooting them between the agricultural buildings. Within the blink of an eye they squirted out onto the north end of the track beside the portable stage that would roll into position at the center of the grandstand for the evening performance once the races were over.

"And now heading out onto the track for the tenth and final heat of the night..."

Pattie's knuckles turned white as she bobbed and weaved the cart as close to the tarmac apron at the base of the stands as she could get, and Jenna bit hers at the announcement Chase was on his warm up lap.

Being the final race of the final night, the crowds were too much even for Pattie's impressive skills and she finally had to admit defeat. "Looks like this is as close as we get gals." She hopped off and pointed to the closest side entrance leading inside the grandstand building. "You'll have better luck cutting through there than you will fighting the crowd out here."

Jenna was already on the move. "Thanks. I'll meet you guys on the other side."

Without giving her eyes time to adjust Jenna blasted through the doorway, nearly wiping out a security guard in her haste.

"Hey lady, where's the fire? Slow down before you hurt somebody!"

Concession kiosks, standup bars, and racing fans hoping for a better view on the indoor monitors, blurred into a wash of color and sound as Jenna sprinted through the lower concourse.

She could hear the security guard's feet hitting the concrete behind her but didn't risk looking back. She was halfway there and could make out the light of the exit she needed near the opposite end when the announcer's voice boomed through the speakers.

"*The wagons are taking their positions at the barrels...*"

Oh no! Wait please, I'm almost there!
"Hey you! Lady! I mean it. Slow down now!"

"*Ladies and gentlemen, as we all know, barrel position at this level of competition can be critical, but don't let that fool you tonight. If Chase Donavan's luck holds, coming off the number four barrel won't keep him out of contention. Let's face it folks, this young man has been sitting on u-shaped shoes all week...*"

Jenna's pounding heart filled with dread and

visions of last time churned her stomach. She started to pray and ran harder; her arms pumping, pushing her burning lungs to their limit and driving a knife of pain into her side.

Chase had come off the four barrel the night of his crash.

Unable to slow her momentum, she turned her body at the last second and slammed into the wall leading to the exit and took the stairs back up to the apron two at a time. As her feet hit ground level, she bounced on her toes trying to see around the people in front of her to the wagons just ahead.

"Outriders are in position..."

"No!" Past the point of caring about anything but getting to Chase, Jenna plowed into the crowd using their arms and shoulders to launch herself forward in a crazed bid for the infield.

She collided into the guard rail twenty feet down the track from the starting barrels and leaned out as far as she could. There he was! Jenna's cupped her hands and lifted them toward her face to call his name just as the Klaxton bell sounded the start of the race drowning her out.

185

"Aannnnd they'rrrre off!"

~*~*~

"Yah!" Chase snapped the lines and felt the adrenaline shoot through his system. His hands worked the leather and his body shifted, matching the rhythm of his powerhouse team of four thoroughbreds without conscious thought.

Deafened by the thundering hooves and rush of blood pounding in his ears he relied on his peripheral vision and his gut to gage his proximity to the other wagons. Missing one of them, or the eight men on horseback, all charging for the narrow bottleneck leading to the open track would spell certain disaster.

Mitch Hanson spun off the number one barrel and shot out a split second ahead of the pack. Tom Slater and Walt Burly, clearing barrels two and three, were right behind him. Wedging in tight, they cut off all but a precariously tight squeeze on the outside rail for Chase.

In that moment, Chase was his father's son, hearing the mantra he grew up on over everything else.

Hesitate, you're too late.

Chase gave a quick tug on one line signally his lead to go for the slot and asked for a burst of speed from the others with another sharp slap of the lines above their backs.

They didn't let him down. As his team surged by on the outside, gaining the advantage into the quarter turn, Chase could've shook hands with Mitch.

The breath off Mitch's lead pair heated his neck down the backstretch and into the three-quarter turn. Knowing his rival was in striking distance of him Chase glanced back to see if his outriders were in range.

They had to cross close enough on his heels for a clean run. He could see one but not the other. He shifted trying for a better look and went wide, giving Mitch the opening he needed to get past him.

"Damn it!" Frustrated at his mistake Chase flipped the wheel horse lines between his teeth and shot forward on his seat, putting all his attention on his lead team and their lines. It was them who'd set the pace and the others were more than capable of keeping up even bringing the thirteen-hundred pound wagon along for the ride.

Bracing his right foot on the edge of the wagon body Chase gave their lines a mighty snap and called for more. "Yah! Yah!"

Head to head he and Mitch flew out of the three-quarter turn, both teams thundering like a pair of locomotives on steroids for the final turn.

Not willing to make the same mistake twice, Chase shot a look over his shoulder before the turn and grinned around the leather in his mouth. Both his boys were right behind him, it would be a penalty free run.

With that concern gone, Chase turned his attention forward again and chose his path into the final turn, sliding over until he was hugging the inside rail.

Mitch ghosted up alongside, but remained a full body length behind Chase's team as they rounded the corner heading into the home stretch and the hundred-thousand dollar finish line in front of the cheering grandstand spectators.

"Come on, that's it, give me all you got!" Sweat and excitement rolled off his exuberant team, mixing with the dirt their powerful stride churned up from the track. Chase's cheeks were numb and grit stuck in his teeth as he muttered around the leather between them. "Come on, boys. You got it, just a little more."

Mitch gained half a wagon length and slid in

closer trying to force him to rein in, but Chase was having none of it. In a risky move, few had the guts or skill to pull off this close to the end of a race, Chase maneuvered his own team off the rail toward Mitch's to give himself more running room and block his opponents bid for the lead.

Anger and frustration flashed on Mitch's face as Chase skimmed past and the risk paid off. Mitch had no choice but pull back to correct his trajectory, leaving Chase's team wide open coming home.

They were ten lengths from the finish line but Chase still heard Mitch over the cheering crowd. "JESUS, DONAVAN! YOU REALLY *ARE* A FUCKING WILD MAN!"

At the same moment the big screens came into Chase's view and seeing his image blazoned across them something shifted in his subconscious and suddenly the meaning behind Cam's cryptic words clicked into place.

2008. Four years earlier! The sculpture of him in Jenna's booth was missing his scar too. Chase's mind ran the rest to its logical conclusion. Jenna sculpted everything she saw, always, she might take license with something but she never omitted it.

The damn thing should've been there. Since it wasn't she had to have done that piece before his accident - and long before she took those pictures that day on the ridge.

Jen had told him the truth.

His heart soared, but that loss of focus while bearing down on the finish line cost Chase dearly. In the few feet it took him to connect the dots, Mitch had pushed like a madman until they were neck and neck, running his team and rig to the limit.

Chase didn't hear the sickening crack from Mitch's left rear wheel with his ears. It was instinct that turned his head. But not fast enough to avoid the broken spoke as it flew through the air straight at his face. It hit so hard it sent him hurling off his wagon.

A lightening bolt blast of pain seared across his forehead and the last thing Chase saw before his world went mercifully black was an up close and personal view of the inside track rail as he smashed head-long into it.

Chapter 12

As the two wagons battled down the final stretch, the stands erupted, bringing the screaming crowd to their feet.

On the ground Jenna turned her body to the side and braced one hand on the rail to avoid being crushed by those on the apron as they pushed forward en-masse in the excitement.

As the Hanson rig came along side Chase's, a man several inches taller and twice Jenna's bulk wormed in front blocking her view. She couldn't see a damn thing!

Without a second thought, Jenna cocked her free arm at the elbow and shoved with all her might. "Excuse me, do you mind!" The man twisted and cursed as he was caught up in the wave of humanity swelling around them and disappeared.

Jenna's hands shook as she reestablished her anchor on the bar separating her from the track and bit her lip as she bobbed and weaved trying to get a look at the finish line.

"It's Chase Donavan on the rail coming in hard, with Mitch Hanson hot on his heels! All outriders are there. This race

isn't over yet folks. Come on Calgary.
They can hear you. So let's bring 'em
home right!"

A hole appeared to her left and Jenna dove in planting her feet as she popped up to discover she had a clear view of the track.

She leaned out, willing Chase across the line and prayed. "Almost there, come on Chase!" A hand landed on her shoulder but she didn't look away. "Jen."

Her aunt had yelled right in her ear and Jenna reached up and clutched Kate's hand, grateful she was there.

"Come on Calgary! Let 'em hear you!"

Wagons charging in at full speed filled Jenna's ears; the rattling riggings and jingling harnesses nearly drowning out the announcer. She felt the pounding hooves and bellowing breath of the horses deep in her chest stealing her own as the race came down to the wire.

"And it's Chase Donavan by a hair
winning the hundred-thousand dollar prize

and the hundredth anniversary edition of
the Rangeland Derby here at the Calgary
Stampede; the greatest outdoor show on
earth!"

The grandstand erupted, sending a shockwave of excitement rolling over Jenna as she slammed her free hand against her mouth. Stifling her squeal she blinked her eyes to shut off the tear factory and struggled to drag air down into her paralyzed lungs.

Oh thank you God, he made it.

Her whole body quaked in the comforting circle of Kate's arms and her knees were so weak she likely would've ended up on her butt without them.

The wagons flew by and Jenna lost sight of Chase's as Mitch stood up and pulled back hard, bracing both feet against the front of his rig to rein in the several thousand pounds of horsepower for their cool down lap. The other two drivers coming in behind did the same and the outriders all stood in the stirrups easing their mounts down from their supercharged run.

A chill shot up Jenna's back. Something didn't sound right. Turning her head her heart leapt into her throat. The fourth wagon - Chase's wagon -

wasn't slowing down.

As it fishtailed around the first turn the reason became terrifyingly obvious. The horses weren't slowing down, because no one was there to pull back on their lines.

Jenna broke from her aunt's embrace and blasted over the rail onto the track only to be pinned in a beefier pair of arms belonging to track security. "Hold on there! What the hell do you think you're doing?"

"Hold on folks, we appear to have a rogue wagon on the track."

"Chase!" Jenna squirmed and struggled, swinging them both until she could see the finish line in the settling dust. Where was he?

"Chase!"

A shadow on the far rail caught her eye and Jenna screamed.

"CHASE! NO!"

"His condition has stabilized but we're keeping him sedated for now."

194

Jenna held JT's gnarled hand in hers and felt the sting of tears in her own eyes as one trailed down his drawn face. "Guess that's a blessing for now." He drew a long breath then squeezed her fingers. "What about his back?"

The doctor gestured for them to sit down and perched on the edge of the waiting room table in front of them. "It could've been far worse. With his previous history, Mr. Donavan was very lucky we were able to salvage the repairs to his lower lumbar area and the prognosis is good." He rubbed his brow and blinked as though banishing the fatigue he had to be feeling after several hours in the operating room. "That doesn't mean he hasn't got a long road ahead of him - and his racing days are over - but with time and rest he'll be able to walk again."

JT released the breath he'd been holding with a shudder. "Thank God for that." He sat up and patted Jenna's hand. "We'll have him back on the ranch before you know it. Some fresh air and hard work—"

The doctor shook his head. "I wouldn't count on that happening any time soon Mr. Tuttle. He's going to have to take it easy for quite a while. Hard manual labor is out of the question for the foreseeable future. At least until we're certain the area around his spine is completely stable. I'm sorry." He got to his feet and glanced at the clock. "You folks should head on home and get some rest. He's in good hands here and I promise we'll call if anything changes before morning. You can come back then and see him. With luck he might even be awake."

Long shadows slid along the walls of the sleeping ward and the soles of the doctor's shoes squeaked in the deserted hallway as he made his way to the elevator. No one spoke until the doors closed behind him.

Completely drained, Jenna stared at the door to Chase's room located directly across from the waiting area she and JT had called home for the last thirty hours.

Panic, guilt, anger and helplessness had taken their toll during that time but she wasn't going anywhere until Chase opened his eyes, and she knew JT wasn't either.

Once they'd gotten past that milestone, she'd deal with the other fear churning in her stomach. *What if he slams the door in your face again?*

"Here's your coffee."

Jenna looked up to find Kate standing there with three cups of Tim Horton's coffee balanced in her hands. It was two o'clock in the morning. Where had she come up with that? At her questioning look, Kate shrugged and handed one over then passed another to JT, who immediately took a big gulp. "Woman you're a saint."

Kate's blush took Jenna off guard but JT's answering one totally shocked her. Auntie Kate and JT?

"Did the doctor come by while I was gone?"

JT had the cup to his lips again so Jenna answered. "He did, and he said Chase is stable but won't be on his feet or back to work on the ranch for quite a while. He's going to need a lot of rest and a lot of physiotherapy."

Kate sank into the seat next to JT and looked between them. "Oh dear, can the ranch afford to loose him right now?"

JT shrugged. "He won the hundred grand fair and square. Tape showed he didn't come off the wagon until he'd crossed the finish line and track officials were able to corral Jared's team so no harm came to the horses, thank heavens."

Jenna started running numbers in her head. "But after Jared's cut, will it be enough do you think...at least for a while?"

"Once the bank chews up their share, we

should still be all right for a while." Leaning back, he pulled his hat down over his eyes and muttered to himself. "Don't know what we'll do after that, but...."

The room faded as reality dawned. Jenna may have been too quick to assume he'd come through before so he would now too. Last time he'd fought against horrendous odds to do it but only had to deal with getting better. But now, the thought he could actually loose the ranch might be enough to make him give up. She knew what his home meant to him.

Lost in thought she didn't notice that her companions had given into their exhaustion. Kate and JT were leaning against each other, one snoring softly; the other mumbling in his sleep. A brief smile graced Jenna's chapped lips. They looked like an old married couple; as different as night and day, but somehow right.

Jenna watched the clock tick the hours away until the sun poked in the window at the far end of the corridor and the nursing station came to life.

For the third time in fifteen minutes she was drawn to her feet and found herself across the hall staring in at Chase's prone figure.

She squeezed her eyes tight to block out the

fact there'd been no change and a movie montage of scenes from the ridge, and what they'd shared that day, played across her mind and brought a quiver to her lip.

Chase's face full of sunshine and life as he charmed the wild mustang into his arms, the fire in his eyes as he gazed at her naked breasts; the wind lifting his hair, creating a halo of black silk around his face. And the tender heat she'd felt under his touch and the explosion of passion they'd shared because of it.

Jenna leaned her forehead against the cold glass and sucked in a shaky breath.

Chase please, wake up. I don't care if you do send me packing again, I can't take not knowing if the man I love is alive and well or not.

The man I love.

Jenna exhaled slowly and opened her eyes. Who had she been trying to kid? Not only *did* she love Chase, she'd never stopped loving him. A peace settled over her, pulling a wave of determination along behind it.

Suddenly, it no longer mattered whether they'd be able to go on from here or not, she was going to do everything in her power to help him anyway. Her heart demanded it.

199

Jenna lifted her head and pulled her lip out from between her teeth. She may not be able to do much about his physical recovery at the moment; only time and patience could do that, but like hell would she stand around and watch him go through this for a second time, only to lose everything.

There had to be a way to make sure he'd still have a home to go to when he got out of here. Didn't there?

Something caught her eye and Jenna's breathing hitched. Did he just move? She squinted through the glass and saw Chase's hand shift and his wrist turn, as though the tubes in his arm annoyed him. She held her breath and clenched her fists wanting to be certain she wasn't imagining things.

Then his head rolled to the side and his face crumpled in a grimace beneath the thick bandage wrapped around his head and she heard him groan. Jenna's heart started to pound both elated he was moving and suddenly fearful so she stayed rooted to the spot, her courage of a minute before wavering.

At least she did until his eyelids started to flutter and her resolve to face him no matter what fled. With her back against the wall next to his door and out of sight from the window, Jenna squeezed her eyes tight and took several deep breaths. She may have to come to terms with the possibility of them going their separate ways eventually, but she couldn't face him making it a reality now.

Coward.

"Jenna-Lynn? You okay?"

How JT snuck up on her without her hearing his boots clunking on the floor, she'd never know, and having him witness her moment of weakness heated her face by several degrees. "Yah...uh, I think he's waking up...."

The raised brow he shot her put Jenna in mind of being caught in the back seat of a car on prom night. She couldn't be dishonest then either. "I...I'm scared he's going to react like he did last time." The last few words came out with a warble so she paused and it came out a whisper instead. "I know I'm an idiot, but I can't help it, JT, I love him and I don't want to lose him a second time."

"Jenna honey, now you listen to me." His callused thumb wiped a tear from her face. "You were nothing but a child then and so was he. And I can tell you something else. He regretted what he did last time more than you can imagine and he will now too if you let it happen again."

What? Jenna's jaw dropped. Let it happen? Is

201

that what she'd done?

JT chucked her chin to close her mouth and smiled. "You gotta think like a horse and bring him to you."

"A horse? What?"

"Yah, a horse." JT nodded at Chase's door. "That's a cowboy lying in there. And everybody knows a cowboy likes a filly with some spirit, you know, one that won't just knuckle under and let him win without first pounding some ground rules of her own into his thick head."

"But—"

"No buts about it. He's gonna need all of us to help him get through the days ahead, and that's a fact. And if you think I'm going to shower his ass with tender loving care, hmph, you can just forget that." He reached for the door handle then looked at her and winked. "That'd be your job - if you want it."

Want it? Of course she wanted it but something else had Jenna's mind sifting through JT's words, a hint she was missing something important nagging in the back of it.

Wait. Her job? A domino fall of thoughts aligned in Jenna's mind and with a squeal she grabbed JT's face by his whiskers and kissed him.

"JT! You're a genius."

"What in tar-nation...I am?"

Excitement lit a fuse under Jenna and her limbs started to tingle. Why hadn't she thought of this before? "Yes. You. Are." She punctuated each word with another peck on his beet red cheek. His scrunched up expression made Jenna laugh out loud for the first time in days. "A cotton-pickin', rootin' tootin' genius!"

He absently rubbed his cheek where her lips had been. "The hell you say."

"Yup, the hell I say." Itching to put her idea to the test, she tilted her head toward the door and pointed her finger. "Now you keep that cowboy in there under wraps and cross your fingers, okay?"

"What's going on—"

Jenna spun on her heel and answered over her shoulder as she hurried to set her scheme in motion. "I can't say yet, but believe me, if this works, you'll be the first to know."

On a mission now, Jenna shook Kate awake and tugged on her arm. "Auntie, wake up."

"Huh? Jen?"

"Come on, up you get. I have an idea, but I need you and Pattie to help, no questions asked. Okay?"

Kate sat up and rubbed the sleep from her eyes, smearing her mascara beyond hope in the process. "Is it devious or sneaky?"

Jenna face broke into a grin. "Both."

Kate grinned back. "Then what are we waiting for? Let's get this show on the road!"

The next guy that pounded a nail into Chase's head was going to get his ass kicked.

He was in a hospital for crying out loud. You'd think a man could get a bloody aspirin around here.

"Hey boy, you coming out of that drug-fog yet?"

JT's voice went off like a gong in his skull, but Chase was glad to hear it anyway. After drifting in and out, wondering if he was having flashbacks, or if he really had ended up back in the hospital again, he needed some clarity.

He vaguely recalled a doctor telling him he was going to be okay - eventually, but this was the first moment he'd been able to hang on to without sinking back into the shadows. Still he wished JT would keep it down a bit. "Do you have to yell?"

"If I was yelling son, there'd be a whole lot

more nurses running in here...wait a minute. They're kinda cute. Not a bad idea boy."

Chase willed one eyelid to lift off its hitching post and hoped it looked bad enough to quell JT's dubious sense of humour. "Are you trying to kill me? Really?"

"Oh, quit your whining. You're breathing aren't ya?"

The strain carved into his friend's face and the slump of his shoulders sobered Chase up. How long had JT been here anyway? "Yah, I am. Not sure I'll appreciate that fact for a while, but, yah, I am. How long have you been here?"

JT picked up his mood shift and responded in kind. "Never mind about that and so help me, if you ever scare the bejesus outta me like this again, you're gonna wish you weren't breathin'. We clear on that? Only reason you skated through again is because you got serious horse shoes stuck up your butt, boy."

JT looked like a rooster whose hen house had been raided and Chase wanted to laugh but it hurt too much. He was also humbled at the crusty ranch-hand's show of concern. JT truly was the father of his heart. "You got it old man. Believe me; I'm not willing to chance it again."

JT snorted to cover the extra shine in his eye. "That's first lick of sense I've heard outta you in ages."

Chase looked over JT's shoulder at the door and lost his train of thought as the face he wanted to see the most floated to the surface - had he been dreaming? Or had Jenna really been here?

As if tripping through his thoughts, JT answered his question. "You scared the pants off all of us, but none worse than Jenna. Until an hour ago, she hadn't left the hospital since they brung you in."

The events of the last several days crashed down on Chase and he began to wish they'd knock him out again. Out on the midway his judgment had been no better than the last time he'd made an arbitrary decision about their relationship and gave her no say in it. Part of him was over the moon she'd been here and another wondered why she'd bothered in the first place after the way he'd treated her.

God he'd been an idiot.

"You're lucky she was, after you being a colossal idiot and all."

Chase frowned and the edge of his bandage crept into his field of vision. "Did they run a wire from my head to yours while I was out or what?"

"Hell no. You think I want to know what's rolling around that head of yours?"

Chase looked away. "No. No, you don't."

JT held his peace for all of ten seconds then cleared his throat. "Forgive me for pushing when you barely got your boots back under you, but I have to ask. Are you gonna be a horse's ass again when it comes to that girl?"

A shard of ice settled in Chase's gut and he couldn't bring himself to look JT in the face because he simply didn't know. Was it fair to expect her to forgive him again?

How could he ask her to give him another chance now?

The silence in the room weighed heavy and finally JT couldn't take it anymore. "Boy, you know I love you like a son, but I gotta tell ya, you are one dumb son-of-a-bitch if you send her down the road again."

Chase heard the feet of JT's chair scrape the floor and saw him head for the door out the corner of his eye but still didn't know what to say.

"Chase how many chances at happiness do you think one person gets?" He opened the door but didn't look back. "I'll tell you one thing; I'd switch boots with you in a heartbeat for a second chance like that. Last thing you want is to wake up one day to discover the years have passed you by leaving you nothing but old and alone. You think on that for a while. I'll be back later to check on you."

Chase found it hard to swallow after the door swung shut. He'd never considered that JT might have lost his heart to someone at some earlier point in his life. He always seemed to be a bachelor by choice. Apparently there was a lot more to JT than any of them had been aware of.

The picture he'd painted didn't sit well with Chase. Seeing himself through the same lens showed him how much he stood to lose. But did he dare hope Jenna might be willing to give them another chance?

He glanced around the room at all the monitors and equipment attached to him and forced himself to go back to four years earlier. Something he'd gotten very good at not doing and not because of what he'd gone through. It was remembering the pain and shock on Jenna's face that twisted his insides whenever he did.

Why, because even though he thought he was being noble at the time, no matter how he sliced it, JT was right. He'd been a colossal idiot. He hadn't even considered giving their relationship a chance to weather his injury last time around.

A mistake he swore he wasn't going to make again.

God and Jenna willing.

For a man who could get a wild horse to eat out of his hand, Chase was having the devils own time getting the woman he loved to trust him. She'd shown up once a week over the last five weeks, always with her aunt or someone else in tow and only stayed a short time.

It didn't take a rocket scientist to figure out she was avoiding being alone with him, when all he could think about was having her in his arms again.

In fact with his body on the mend he caused more than one professional medical worker to blush when they woke him up for his meds in the morning only to find a rather large tent sticking up from the sheets.

The whole situation was driving him up a wall.

JT wasn't helping any either. No matter how much he tried to pump information about what Jenna was up to the rest of the time the old mule wouldn't budge. He wouldn't even tell him about what was going on at home.

The only useful tidbit of information he'd gotten was that Jared had wired his share of the winnings into the Flying D's account and the bank had siphoned off the back payments on the mortgage so they were current and the pressure was off for now.

"We're going to miss you Mr. Donavan." His usual day nurse, Wendy, pushed a wheelchair up beside Chase's bed. "I'm sure you can't say the same of us, but anyway, I'm just glad you're well enough to go home."

Chase gave the rolling metal contraption a dirty look. "Can't I use my canes?"

"Now come on. You know the rules. The only way anybody gets off this ward is to roll off - hospital protocol number twenty-two seventeen. So suck it up, get in, and enjoy the ride." Wendy angled the chair and hit the brake.

Chase lifted himself off the bed with his arms and carefully lowered himself into the hated thing. "I was about to say I'd miss the nursing staff, if not the hospital, but I may have to reconsider my position on that."

Wendy gave his ear a tweak from behind and giggled. "Hey, you're still at my mercy there buddy, so I'd watch it if I were you. Otherwise I may feel it professionally necessary to order a thorough pipe cleaning before deeming you ready to go."

JT came into the room and winked at the nurse. "The prince of charm strikes again I see."

"Hey, I was being nice. She's the one threatening bodily harm."

"I'd say what she's threatening has more to do with bodily function than harm, and the last time I checked nurses don't give enemas to departing patients as a matter of course. So you musta done something to rile her up."

Wendy giggled and released the brake on Chase's chair. "I can see I'm delivering you into capable hands."

"More like chucking me to the wolves."

"Hey, we gonna need to call the roto-rooter brigade in after all?"

Chase's pretense of pouting ended at the desk, when his nurse surprised him by crouching beside him and taking his hand in hers. "All kidding aside, the progress you've made in such a short time is an inspiration to a lot of people around here. We all want to see you go home now and live a long and happy life. God bless you Chase."

Chase lifted her hand and brushed her knuckles

with his lips in gratitude. "I couldn't have done what I have without the great care I got from all of you. Please accept my heartfelt thanks and pass it on to the others would you?"

"Sure will." She stood up and handed an envelope to JT. "These are the prescriptions the doctor filled out for him. You'll need to have them filled on your way home."

JT accepted it, and with his own thanks, headed them down the hall to the elevator and freedom.

Chase was going home to live a long life. Whether it'd be a happy one or not depended completely on a certain skittish little filly.

Thank goodness they'd stopped to fill those prescriptions. Chase was going to need a double dose when they finally got home. "Since when did this road get so damn rough?"

"What are you talking about? Road's the same as it's always been."

"Then I hope we can afford to do something about it before winter."

JT's mustache twitched and the creases of his laugh lines got deeper for the third time since leaving the hospital. "What's so funny?"

JT averted his face, stirring Chase's suspicions. The telltale red where he rubbed at his neck, and the fact the man was squirming in his seat ramped them up even more.

"Funny? Who says anything's funny?"

"Me. That's who. I know you, old man, and right now you're up to something."

JT busied himself adjusting the rearview mirror. "No idea what would make you think that. Maybe you need one of them pills."

"I don't need any pills. Well, yes I do, but—"

They rounded the last bend, and broke out of the trees bringing the ranch into view. Suddenly Chase's mouth was too busy hanging open to form the rest of his comment.

They crossed under the timber-pole arch into the main yard where a crowd of people stood waiting under a huge banner. There had to be at least a hundred of them. "JT, what's all this?"

JT was really squirming in his seat now and had a silly grin on his face. "Read the sign, genius!"

The truck rolled to a stop in front of the house and Chase took a closer look.

The silhouette of a horse's head rearing took up the middle. Above it, the Flying D name and brand were written in letters and symbols that looked like rope. Both of these things he could understand. It was the words marching across the bottom, as though someone had written them with a paint brush, saying 'Future Home of the Artist's Ride North' that had him baffled.

What the hell was an Artist's Ride North?

Before he could get the question out, JT opened his door and handed Chase his canes. "Thought you might prefer these over that metal monstrosity in the back."

Touched by his friend's thoughtfulness, Chase took them and carefully made his way out of the truck. "Thanks." JT stayed at his side, and helped steady him as they crossed the yard. Several people looked like they were ready to burst their skins but not a single person made a sound.

"So boy, ain't you gonna say something?"

The atmosphere was charged with so much anticipation, he started to worry the guy from that show 'Punked' was about to jump out in his face. "Uh, I would, if I had a clue what to say."

"Wow, that's a first. You must've cracked your melon harder than I thought."

The voice didn't belong to a TV host but it was a surprise none-the-less, one straight out of his

214

misbegotten youth. "Cohen?"

"No worries cousin, I may only be a Shaman-in-training, but I can still fix you up."

A hand the size of a lot of people's feet landed on Chase's shoulder and he could've sworn a flash of warmth eased the clenched muscles in his lower back. Then it was gone.

Chase smiled at his sometimes mentor, most times cohort. "Man I must be in dire straights to drag you down off your mountain."

Cohen pointed in the general direction of the corral with his chin. "Nah, I'm just here for the beer."

"The beer?" Chase must've had a stunned look on his face because his cousin's six-foot four, frame shook with laughter and a wide grin lit up his ageless face.

Chase looked over and, sure enough, a makeshift bar, complete with beer taps, had been set up over there. What the hell was going on?

JT's squirming had turned into a full blown case of ants-in-the-pants. "Cohen, you gonna get on with it, or what?"

Cohen frowned at JT's prodding, then appeared to take pity on him and raised his voice so everyone in the vibrating crowd could hear. "Congratulations,

Chase my man, you and me are about to go into business together."

What? Cohen cared about as much for the outside world as Chase did about underwater basket weaving. He might not be on 'Punked' but Chase was definitely in some kind of twilight zone and it was making his aching head spin. "Going into business? What are you talking about?" He looked between his cousin and JT with growing confusion. "Would somebody please tell me what's going on?"

"Okay, okay, cuz, but you're taking all the fun out of it." Cohen led him toward the others but kept his voice lowered as they walked. "Chase, a lot of us know the D's been struggling."

Chase started to put on the brakes. "Hold it right—"

"Whoa, chill. Before you go getting yourself all lathered, shut up and listen." He tilted his head toward the group ahead. "These people are your friends and neighbors. People your family has been there for through thick and thin. Now they want to be there for you. It's what we do in this neck of the woods and always have.

JT piped up. "Amen." Cohen glanced at him sideways and JT bristled. "What? I'm just agreeing with ya is all."

Chase caught Cohen's wink and did his best to hide a smile. "Okay, I get the message. So when do we get to the 'what is all this' part?"

A tall distinguished looking man stepped up and cleared his throat. "I think that's my cue." In three long strides he breached the ground between them and stuck his hand out to Chase. "Hi, Mr. Donavan, it's nice to meet you. My name's Doug, and on behalf of myself and several of the artists from around here, I want to tell you how excited we all are about this venture."

Chase's headache was growing by the minute. "What venture?"

As the words left his mouth the barn door opened and out rode several Nakota on horseback, everyone in full native costume and grinning ear to ear.

As the procession slowly rode up and formed a semicircle under the banner, Cohen finally answered his question. "Welcome to the future home of the Artist's Ride North, a division of Flying D Enterprises. A place where twice a year in the spring and fall, the neighboring Nakota nation will get all gussied up and stage historically correct reenactments for paying artists to photograph as references and inspiration for their work."

A cheer rose up from everyone and the riders had to tighten their hold to keep the horses from spooking.

"Flying D Enterprises? Paying artists?" Chase leaned harder on his canes as the picture became clearer. Was it possible? Could this be a long-term answer to his financial trouble? "Cohen? How much money are we talking about here?"

Cohen chuckled and swatted him hard enough to make Chase wobble. "Dude, we're talking enough green to cover the mortgage on this chunk of dirt for a full year, every year." Then his Shaman-in-training cousin broke into an awkward rendition of a butter-churn dance and started chanting. "That's right. That's right. Yo money troubles is outta sight."

JT swiped his hat off his head and clamped Chase in a man-hug, complete with shoulder slapping and grumbling, while friends, neighbors and strangers gathered around, filling his little valley with laughter and hope. "JT? Whose idea was all this?"

Chase hadn't realized his question had gone beyond JT's ears, until he sensed the change in energy around him. Cohen's hip circles slowed to a stop, riders steadied their mounts and a hush resettled over everyone.

JT retrieved his hat and waved it toward the open barn door without answering.

Chase's turn was less than graceful with his canes, and when he saw her, he'd have landed on his ass if Cohen hadn't planted his palm between his shoulder blades.

He gulped and blinked to make sure she was really there and he wasn't just seeing what he wanted to. Until this moment, he hadn't allowed himself to admit he'd been looking for her in every face or how empty his homecoming had been when she wasn't there. "Jen?"

Jenna had worked herself into a serious state watching from the barn for the big reveal. She'd argued against Cohen's idea to surprise Chase in public and seeing the blank look on his face now, she still wasn't sure who'd been right.

She had no idea what he was thinking. She'd barely even spoken to him, at least not while he was conscious, since they argued on the midway, for goodness sake.

When the inspiration struck her that night at the

hospital it had seemed like the perfect solution.

Now, the more she thought about it, the more she worried how he might resent her meddling in his affairs - and the bigger the angry hornet's nest in her belly got.

"Jen?"

He started to move toward her and the sun glinted off his canes, momentarily blinding her. Moon Dancer stuck his head over the gate of his stall and pushed his nose against her shoulder as if to say: *What are you doing making him come to you, you ninny?*

Jenna blinked and realized the horse was right, but the closer she got the larger her heart swelled and the more her nerves jumped.

She came to a stop a few feet from him and Chase's blank mask became one of disbelief. His voice cracked and a hint of wariness surfaced in his eyes. "You did all this? It was all your idea?"

Her arms ached, she wanted to hold him so bad and her voice didn't sound much better than his when she spoke. "Yes."

He closed the gap in one step and threw one of his canes to the ground so he could pull her in tight to his chest. "After what a bastard I—"

A strangled cry escaped Jenna and she tangled

her fingers in his hair as though afraid he'd vanish if she didn't hold on tight enough. "It doesn't matter if you don't want me—"

Chase buried his face in the crook of her neck and filled his lungs with her sweet scent. "I'm so sorry Jen, I'll understand if you can't forgive me—"

Jenna pressed her body against his wanting nothing more than to feel him against her one last time. "All I want is for you to be happy because—"

Chase rubbed his cheek against hers. "But if you decide to leave I can't let you go without telling you—"

Their lips found each other and their breath mingled as they spoke their hearts in unison. "I love you."

Their gazes locked, each registering the truth of their words shining back at them. The only sound was their labored breath and the wind tickling the cottonwood leaves in the yard.

Jenna broke the spell first. "You do?"

Chase smiled and kissed the end of her nose. "I do."

Cohen's shadow blocked the sun as he wrapped his arm around Chase and stage-whispered in his ear. "Uh, cuz. I think she's supposed to say that part first."

Chase's frown didn't quite reach his eyes and Jenna didn't bother stifling her giggle. She'd forgotten how outrageous this guy was.

"You *are* going to cop with the proposal bit, right? So, I'm just saying, it's the girl who says the 'I do' first." Cohen glanced over his shoulder and bobbed his head up and down. "Right?"

A ripple of laughs and agreements ran through the circle of happy faces and Cohen turned his attention back to them. "Okay. So let's have it."

Chase pasted an overly innocent look on his face, and Jenna felt the muscles in his stomach clench against a laugh. "Have what?"

Cohen shook his head sending his warrior braids flapping and threw his hands in the air. "To think the same blood runs through my veins."

Jenna couldn't hold off her giggles and earned a tweak in the ribs from Chase for her lack of restraint.

Cohen bent closer. "No worries Chase my man. Like I said earlier, I got your back." Next thing Jenna knew, the man had planted his hands on his knees and leaned in so their three faces were only inches apart as though he were the quarterback and they were his football huddle. "Now Chase, look at Jenna."

Chase's tremor was [...]
was cracking. "Okay."

"So, you do plan to ask this [...]
sacrifice the rest her natural born li[...]
marriage, yah?"

Chase's eyebrows hit his hairline and [...]
opened his mouth. "I—"

"'Kay. Good. Jenna, you poor thing, are you [...]
certain you want to spend the rest of the time you
have on this earth waking up to that ugly mug every
morning?"

Chase stuck his lip out and his puppy-dog
expression sent Jenna into a fit of laughter. "When
he pulls that face, how can I resist."

Cohen clapped his hands and stood up breaking
the huddle. Then he raised his hands and spoke to
the crowd. "Okay people. This wedding's in the
bag."

On JT's muttered 'bout damn time' a round of
congratulations and cheer erupted filling Jenna's
body with tingles from head to toe. She looked up
into the love and happiness shining on Chase's
handsome face, hardly daring to believe this
moment was real.

A month ago, he would've run for the hills
behind them rather than have something as private

y. Now he
rrounding

e from his
onding burst
ndings.

getting worse and his face
lovely woman to
e to you in
he

her belly
s, I'll marry

A warning growl deep in his throat started her laughing again. "I love you Chase Donavan. I always have."

Chase swept in and captured her mouth with his, devouring every sigh and moan with relish. His tongue danced with hers until her toes curled in her boots and she sorely wished they were alone.

"Oh God, Jen, I never stopped loving you either."

Jenna sighed. She couldn't be happier. Chase was in her arms, both he and his home safe, and they were about to start their life together. Jenna couldn't think of a single thing that could ruin this perfect moment.

At least not until a shadow passed over them and Jenna opened her eyes to Marla Gibson's talon of a fingernail tapping Chase's shoulder.

"Is this a good time to bring up your breach of contract?"

"It clearly states in subsection C, paragraph four, that any alteration of features or extraneous markings or embellishments to any area of the body, without the express written consent of the party of the first part - that would be me - puts the party of the second part - which would be you - in direct breach of this legal and binding contract."

Chase had had enough of feeling like the whole world suddenly spoke Greek and was in no mood to put up with Marla Gibson. Shifting his body and pulling Jenna around to the side, he struggled not to snarl. "I'm only going to say this once. Ms. Gibson. Cut the crap and make your point."

"Oh Marla, drop the act before he kicks our asses off his land." A flurry of energy burst past the bar at the corral and came to a stop on Chase's other side.

Marla crossed her arms and leaned back on one foot only to have her high heel sink into the ground bringing her close in height to Tamra. "I am never dramatic Tamra dear."

"Yah whatever, like he said cut to the chase." Tamra rolled her eyes at Marla's smug look. "Not *him* Chase - *the* chase."

After the whole 'Wild' campaign thing, Marla wasn't the most popular person on his list but Chase did have to give her credit for not coming out of her shoes as she worked to pull them free. "Tinkerbelle, why don't we save us all a lot of pain and you tell me what she's talking about."

"You want the down and dirty, here it is. You took a wheel spoke to the face in the accident resulting in that scar on your forehead."

Jenna tensed under his arm. "And."

"Scars are considered an alteration according to the contract—"

Jenna sprang forward and squared off with Tamra before Chase could gain his balance and stop her. "Of all the ridiculous things I've heard in my life, that takes the cake."

Tamra leaned in and planted her hands on her hips, mirroring Jenna's stance and got up in her face. "Couldn't agree more."

"If you think—" Tamra's words sunk in and Jenna sputtered. "You do?"

Cohen sauntered up in the ensuing silence and poked Chase. "Who's the elf?"

Marla, back on her spiked heels, started to laugh. "Okay ladies, break it up. I've had my fun." She patted Tamra's shoulder then took Jenna's clenched fist and handed her back to Chase. "Here's the deal, handsome. Your pretty face, although admittedly more rugged in its own way, is no longer suitable to represent *'Wild'* cologne."

Before anyone could get a word in, she raised her hand and clucked her tongue. "Ah ah. Let me finish." She paused and got a twinkle in her eye. "And now boys and girls, here's where you discover the true power of a brilliant agent.

"I have personally negotiated the following deal on your behalf. In exchange for use and all rights in perpetuity to the original image of you prior to the aforementioned alteration, Evian agrees to release you from any further contractual obligation."

Chase would've bellowed if Jenna hadn't first. "Are you kidding? Chase signs away everything and gets nothing. Where's the deal in that."

Marla waved her off like she was swatting a mosquito then inspected her manicure. "Oh, guess I forgot mention the two point five million dollar cheque that goes along with the deal."

Jenna's hand slowly reached around behind

grasping for his and Chase was only too glad to oblige, needing something physical to hang onto as his brain processed what his ears just heard.

"That is of course, if you agree."

Cohen cut loose with a 'hell yah you agree cuz, don't be stupid,' followed by a coyote howl which acted like striking a match to dynamite. Everyone started taking at once and the news spread like wildfire through the yard to those out of ear-shot.

Someone yelled 'Yeehaw' and broke open a keg. Somebody else popped open the back of a car and cranked up the stereo, while another got the grill going. Before long the smell of barbeque mingled with people as they started singing and kicking up their heels to the latest country songs.

Chase and Jenna snuck off a little way up the hill behind the house overlooking the yard as the sun sank in the western sky. A golden light bathed the revelers in a soft glow.

Movement near the food tables caught his eye and Chase shook his head as he watched Cohen stalking Tamra across the yard. His poor cousin didn't stand a chance. Tinkerbelle would eat him for breakfast.

From the look of it, Marla was doing her best to convince one of his outriders that the camera would love him and JT was spinning Jenna's Auntie Kate around the dance floor like they were the only people there.

A peace he hadn't known before blanketed Chase as he snuggled Jenna under his arm, pulling her in nice and close and resting his chin on the top of her head. Looking to the sky, he sent a silent thank you to the winds and hoped it found his mother smiling and as happy as he was.

"Look!" Jenna started and pointed to the far ridge where the sun was all but gone.

Chase instantly saw what she had, and a tendril of wonder unfurled in him at the sight.

There, against the purple dusk sky, Thunderhead reared and tossed his mane for several seconds, trumpeting, as his hooves churned the air. Then crashing to the ground the stallion wheeled and led his herd up over the rise, disappearing with the day.

A soft breeze caressed Chase's face and Jenna lifted her lips to his, turning the wonder of the moment to pure magic.

When she spoke her voice was soft and Chase almost missed her question. "What made you decide differently this time?"

He stroked her cheek with his knuckles and

reminded himself he owed a certain cowboy a debt of gratitude he might never be able to pay. "Someone recently told me that saying about loving something and setting it free was a load of bull crap."

Her body stiffened. "What?"

Chase glanced down and smiled at her confused frown. "Yah, he looked me dead in the eye and said that if I ever saw something I wanted more than anything in the world, I should grab on to her ass as tight as I could and hold on."

He could see the wheels turning and smirked. "Then, he said, if we could make it for eight without landing on our faces in the dirt, I should never let her go."

Jenna popped up and swatted at him. "What kind of dumb cowboy logic is that?'

Before she connected he caught her hands and carefully lay back in the tall grass out of everyone's view taking Jenna down with him. "Now look who's the wild one."

Then Chase caught her lips with his and delving deep, held on long past eight.

THE END

Turn the Page for a Preview of an upcoming
Stampede Sizzler

WILLING FOR COWBOY
by
Victoria Chatham

Coming Soon from **Stampede Sizzlers**
WILLING FOR COWBOY
By
Victoria Chatham

Chapter 1

She was thirty years old, for heaven's sake, and traveled around the world a dozen or more times in the last decade. And now she was nervous?

Trisha Parker caught her bottom lip between straight white teeth and mentally shook herself. She'd survived photo shoots on the African veldt, in the Australian outback, the Southern Alps of New Zealand and most recently, Afghanistan. Judging a photography competition in Calgary, Canada at the Greatest Outdoor Show on Earth, deep in the heart of cowboy country, should be a breeze.

Shouldn't it?

Why then, did she have this heavy weight of anticipation hanging over her? She could have refused the invitation, or invented some obscure project but Marla Gibson, once having made up her mind, was not a person to be denied. And now Trisha was in Calgary, waiting for that same Marla Gibson to collect her from the airport.

She checked her watch, having altered it to local Mountain Time after the pilot's in-flight announcement gave the estimated time of arrival, wind speed and weather conditions. Her flight was on time, customs and baggage retrieval had gone without a hitch but there was no sign of Marla.

Typical, Trisha thought, then turned at the sound of her name. At first she couldn't make out who had called her. Then a diminutive figure, resembling a demented pixie, pushed her way to the forefront of a group of people and skipped towards her.

"Hi, Ms. Parker, I'm Tamra," she announced as she grabbed Trisha's luggage and hauled it onto a cart. "Marla's been held up, she's trying to get a new model under contract but the girl definitely has her own ideas. Has some outrageous demands and Marla's tearing her hair out. She said to take you straight to her apartment and she'll join you as soon as the ink is dry. This way."

Oh, Lord, thought Trisha as she listened to Tamra's rapid-fire chatter. A Marla doppelganger.

The chatter continued non-stop as Tamra pointed out one landmark after another along the route into Calgary's downtown core. Trisha silently admitted to herself that it was one of the more friendly downtown skylines she had encountered and far more interesting than she'd expected.

"What's that building?" she asked, pointing towards an ultra modern angular building bristling with steel and glass.

"Our new science centre." Tamra slid easily into the flow of traffic heading into the city. "That's the zoo on the left, and the Bow River right here and we're just cutting through Chinatown. Do you like Chinese food? "

"Yes, and Greek, Italian and Indian, but not necessarily in that order," Trisha answered with a laugh.

"Calgary's pretty cosmopolitan; you'll find all that and more here. But through Stampede we all live on breakfasts."

Tamra stopped the car in front of a garage door, pressed a remote clipped onto the visor and waited for the door to open. Trisha tried to imagine living on breakfast for ten days. Tamra chattered on as she unloaded the car and Trisha followed her into the elevator. She could hardly believe that Marla's assistant was still talking.

"... and I said to her, well it's not really your business and she fired me. Again. Here we are." Tamra flung open a door and Trisha walked into an apartment that momentarily took her breath away.

"I know," said Tamra, hearing Trisha's gasp.

"Everyone has the same reaction when they walk in here. Marla has this great interior designer who was so pleased with this reno he's featured it in loads of magazines. Your room's down here. Has its own en suite. Coffee machine's in the kitchen. Or would you prefer tea? It can brew either. Oh, wine in the fridge. Anything else you'd like?"

Bemused, Trisha sat on the end of a queen sized bed covered in white linens.

"Umm, no, thank you. I think...."

Before Trisha could say what she thought, Tamra wiggled her fingers as a goodbye, said that was alright then, assured her Marla should be with her right away, and disappeared.

Trisha didn't even hear the door close as she fell back on the bed and let the blissful silence wrap around her like an invisible but comfortable blanket.

She opened her eyes at about the same time that Marla walked into the room.

"Well, that was a bitch of a day."

Marla's throaty voice hadn't changed one bit in two years and Trisha couldn't help but grin.

"Hello, Marla. It's good to see you too."

"Oh, hell." Marla pulled Trisha into a rough

hug of welcome. "Don't mind me, I'm being crabby. How was your flight?"

"Took off from Heathrow, landed in Calgary. What more can I say?" Trisha stood up and stretched.

Marla eyed her speculatively. "When did you get so skinny? You look more like you should be in front of the camera, not behind one. Need an agent?"

Trisha hid her sudden flutter of apprehension with a nervous chuckle. "My last assignment rather got the better of me and no, thank you. No agents for me."

Her stomach rumbled, reminding her that it had not been fed for several hours.

"I heard that," Marla said. She hadn't missed Trisha's comment about that last assignment. It piqued her curiosity and she tucked it away in her mental filing cabinet for future reference. "Do you want to eat out or in?"

"Whichever's easiest, but first I'm having a shower."

"Go for it." Marla got to her feet. "Everywhere's going to be crazy with Stampede about to start, but it's still early enough that we should go and get you duded up."

Trisha stuck her head around the bathroom

5

door. "Duded up?"

"Yep, pardner." Marla nodded. She wasn't successful in trying to hide her grin behind a serious expression . "You need cowboy boots, shirt and jeans, and a cowboy hat. I can't possibly take you out on the town unless you are dressed western, unless you think you're too posh for that."

Trisha snorted with unladylike laughter and closed the door.

Trisha couldn't believe the variety and styles of shirts and jeans in the store. Marla flicked through the racks like the professional fashion maven she was and pulled one shirt after another out for Trisha to try on. She ran a practiced glance over Trisha's slim hips and long legs.

"Size ridiculous in a thirty-two inch leg coming up." She added four pairs of jeans to the pile of shirts and pushed Trisha into a changing room. "Start trying that lot on and I'll get you a pair of boots and a hat."

Marla left no room for argument. Trisha picked a black shirt with a small periwinkle blue floral pattern on it. She pulled on a pair of jeans, stiff with newness, and tucked the shirt tail into the waistband

6

and zipped up. Before she could even look at herself, Marla's head appeared over the bat-wing change room doors.

"Nope. Your hair's black and I forgot your eyes are blue. It's too dark for you, you just fade into it. My mistake." Marla rifled through the selection of shirts again. "Try this white eyelet shirt. It's darted so should really show off your waist. Here's a pair of boots, I'll go and find you a belt with a blingy buckle. A girl's got to have bling."

She disappeared again and Trisha peeled out of the dark shirt and poured herself into the white one. She turned to push her way out of the change room then stopped, stunned into immobility by the sight of the cowboy who stood by the store counter.

He had to be at least six foot four inches tall. A vast expanse of crisp white shirt covered his wide shoulders and broad back and did nothing to hide the spectacular biceps in his arms.

His blue jeans hugged his hips and molded around his thighs and butt as if sprayed on. She flexed her fingers and her mind conjured up pictures of what her hands could do to that butt.

Something slammed under her heart and parts of her body she'd almost forgotten belonged to her sprang to immediate attention. Without thinking, she licked her lips. Then, realizing what she had

7

done, she ducked back into the change room. She covered her flaming face with her hands.

Had anyone seen her? She thought not. She prayed not.

She perched on the narrow, slatted seat, built more for holding clothes than a dead weight with rubber legs. Her pulse pounded and her head spun. Her mouth was as dry as the Kandahar dust.

"Pull yourself together, Trisha," she muttered.

She peeked out of the change room once more. Whoever he was, he stood in deep conversation with the clerk. She savoured the sight of him, feeling immature and foolish as her gaze caressed every inch of him. She was acting like a love-struck teenager.

She did not want to feel anything. Must not feel anything. It was so totally wrong.

"Hey, you okay in there?"

Marla's voice brought her back into the here and now. Trisha stood up, pushed her hair out of her eyes and finished fastening the buttons on the white shirt.

Put on a brave face and party on, babe, she told herself. She shouldered her way through the swing doors and Marla looked her up and down.

"Much, much better." She held out a white hat and Trisha placed it on her head, tucking her hair behind her ears. "Now for the boots."

Trisha looked down. The boots Marla had chosen for her were tooled black leather with a silver tip on the toe. She put her right foot into one boot and pushed her foot down.

"Marla, you're amazing," she exclaimed as she put her left foot into the other boot. "These fit perfectly. How do I look?"

"From where I'm standing, you look pretty damn fine to me."

Both women looked up. Trisha swallowed hard.

Mr. Heart-attack-on-legs was giving her a smoldering grey-eyed once over. Trisha straightened up slowly and found an equally impressive front view of the back she had so recently been hyperventilating over. She stared hard at the middle buttons on his shirt and tried to ignore the small nicks and scars she could see on his hand.

He reached out and adjusted the collar on her shirt, then brushed something from her shoulder. It was a barely there touch, yet the heat and strength of his fingers seared her skin through the thin fabric.

She peeked up under the brim of her hat and wished she hadn't. She couldn't tear her eyes away from his. The smart reply her brain produced got lost in transit to her lips. She would have continued to stare numbly at him if Marla, reading her witless expression after one swift glance, hadn't quickly agreed with him.

He nodded at Marla but aimed his slow, mind blowing sexy smile directly at Trisha. He tipped his hat to her and left the store.

Trisha watched him go, every breath in her body trailing after him until she floundered like a fish out of water and gasped to fill her empty lungs.

Marla eyed her with amused curiosity.

"I think that you," she purred, "are definitely in trouble."

Other Stampede Sizzler Titles Currently Available:

Hot For Cowboy by Wynne Holmes
Reckless For Cowboy by Daire St. Denis
Gay For Cowboy by Jade Buchanan
Burn For Cowboy by Jenna Howard

A BANDIT CREEK
PARANORMAL ROMANCE

Shafted

KYMBER MORGAN

Excerpt from:

SHAFTED
A Bandit Creek Paranormal Tale
By
Kymber Morgan

An obnoxious sound polluted the air, loud enough to make Anteros wince. It took to the count of three to realize the annoyingly repetitive groan was coming from him.

That couldn't be good.

Had he gotten drunk with Charon again? His brain cells were sluggish coming back online, but didn't miss the cold cramp of muscles and aching bones currently housing him. Shit, he was probably on the crap end of another of his friend's oh-so-hilarious practical jokes.

The last one entailed a term of servitude to the Furies before he was able to buy his way out of their lair. Given the nature of his indenture, time with them wasn't all bad, but that wasn't the point. No one wanted to piss off a woman created to rip a man's soul from his still breathing body, let alone three of them, so wiggling his way out of that one had been tricky. Was he on the banks of the Styxx this time? Why else would he be so cold? It wasn't

1

like the Underworld had an air conditioning problem or anything. Or worse, had the bastard dumped him on the shores of Acheron, the River of Woe?

A shard of dread lodged in his heart. In either case being a god himself didn't mean there wouldn't be Hades to pay – literally – and Anteros already owed his uncle too much after that last ill fated poker game. Contemplating the consequences made his head spin even worse.

A nudge in his ribs interrupted his conjecture, shooting a spike of warning up his spine. It really didn't matter which of the Underworld Rivers he was languishing beside, anything corporeal enough to touch him was bad news. Here, only the damned, stuck without coin for the Ferryman, had substance. To them anything that might pay their way to the other side, especially some other poor sap's soul, was fair game.

"Hey? Are you…"

Knowing surprise was his best shot, Anteros snaked his arm out and grabbed the prodding limb before it could drag him into the river. Charon had been his friend longer than either could remember, but there was no way he'd give a soul back, even Anteros's, if he ever got hold of it.

With a hard yank and a yelp from the thing, he

pulled his assailant down and flipped his body.

Scissoring his long legs he trapped the other and pinned it beneath his superior mass. A wave of corresponding vertigo hit before his besotted brain caught up to the lighting fast movement.

Keeping his stomach in check wasn't easy, but he'd be damned if some soul-sucking vagrant was going to drag his ass into in that disgusting water, especially hung over.

It took as much determination to open his eyes as it did to beat back the lingering nausea, but he clenched his teeth tighter and forced himself to blink away the blurriness. He needed to see what he was up against before the thing regained its equilibrium.

As his vision cleared, shock drove the remaining miasma away. The thing was hideous! Its upper body was bloated and lumpy, and there were stiff mangled strands where its face should be. Though much smaller than him and vaguely human in shape, it had enormous rubbery feet and red blobs instead of hands. Had they been cut off before the thing died?

Worse yet, it was making a pitiful noise, as though screaming with its mouth sewn shut. It was actually kind of pathetic. Deciding the thing wasn't such a huge threat after all, Anteros began to lift his weight, planning to simply roll it back into the river where it belonged and be done with it.

Before he could get a good hold, the thing jerked violently under him and suddenly every molecule of air in his body evacuated in response to the worst explosion of pain he'd ever experienced in his life. Fireworks shot off, blinding him beneath his puckered eyelids and his breath burst painfully from his insta-paralyzed lungs. His beleaguered stomach filled with acid and his limbs gave out all at once, dropping him to the ground like a stone. Not in all his eons had he felt pain like this. Apparently he wasn't the only one who could use the element of surprise.

The bastard had canned him!

"What the hell do you think you're doing? Are you crazy? God I thought you were hurt. I just wanted make sure you were okay and you freaking attack me!"

With the bells of Hades ringing in his ears, it took a minute for Anteros to realize it wasn't 'Dead Soul Speak' wailing at him, but what sounded suspiciously like the annoying screech of a mortal female.

What was a mortal doing here? He must still be drunk. That was it. He'd heard enough Ambrosia could make you think things were real, which must

4

be true because he could swear the apparition fidgeting a few feet away was really there.

"I'm so sorry. Are you going to be okay? I didn't mean to hurt you, but you caught me off guard when you grabbed me. Scared me, you know?"

Anteros braved another glimpse, cracking one eye open; yup, an ugly one to be sure, but a mortal female nonetheless. She hadn't come any closer probably to stay out of range should he retaliate. Smart girl, but he could hear the genuine regret and concern in her voice.

"Mister? Hey really, are you going to be okay? Should I call for help? A doctor or something?"

His tongue might as well have been coated in cement for all the good it did him. "In fin, unky dorky. Kint you till? Jus gim me a sick to gatch my bret."

"Excuse me I didn't quite get that."

He flopped over onto his back, hoping his lungs would remember what to do with the first full breath of air they'd gotten in what seemed like an eternity, and cleared his throat to try again. "I'm fine, hunky dory. Can't you tell? Just give me a second to catch my…."

The last word formed on his lips, but as his eyes focused, he lost track of what he was saying.

5

He was snared by a pair of green eyes fringed in enough frost to stick their edges together, giving them a disturbing mismatched shape. They were peering at him out of a blotchy pink face, complete with a hint of chapped lips, a runny nose and a mess of icicle spiked hair sticking out in every direction like some frozen parody of Medusa.

She was beautiful.

Huh? Where the Hades had that come from? What in the Nine Hells was wrong with him?

As though struck by a God-bolt, his memory came crashing back and with it the truth of how he ended up here.

He hadn't been drinking with Charon at all. No, he'd been coming in after a particularly painful fix of another of his brother's careless mistakes…. Suddenly the last piece of the puzzle clicked into place, filling him with an overwhelming sense of dread and anger.

The miserable little shit shafted him! *HIS OWN BROTHER!*

He'd barely entered his temple home on Olympus when something behind one of the marble columns had caught his eye. He lived alone, and rarely did any care to visit, so he immediately recognized the movement for the threat it was.

He remembered reaching behind his shoulder

with one hand and bringing his black titanium bow to bear with the other, but not fast enough. Flickering torchlight caught a golden flash flying straight at – no, through – him. Anger turned to bitterness as the memory played across his mind.

As darkness pulled him under, Eros had emerged from the shadows, still holding his own glistening bow, a triumphant grin on his handsome face. Not a moment later their mother had materialized directly behind him, her face void of emotion, but her words had said it all.

"Perfect shot, my son, you've done well."

He'd been shafted all right. The love of Psyche, Eros's wife, had proven too much for his brother, causing his fall to ambro-fever, an irreversible condition many gods developed after an overload of what they personified. The result in Eros's case was him periodically running amok, so drunk on love he couldn't see, let alone shoot straight, willy-nilly nailing any poor sucker who got in his path.

It had fallen to Anteros as the God of Requited Love to run damage control by canceling out his brother's diamond-tipped silver arrows with his opposing obsidian-tipped lead ones. Instead of being the final reckoning for those who deliberately preyed on the hearts of others, it became his job to save mortals suddenly in love against their will with people who would never love them in return. Anteros was the only one able to free Eros's shooting-spree victims but it meant absorbing their heartache as his own to do it.

And what thanks did he get for spending the last several centuries drawing in and carrying the pain of all those hearts? His beloved brother, the one at fault in the first place, shot him - and on their mother's orders no less! And not with just any arrow either. No, it had to be one of his thrice cursed golden ones. His fate was sealed.

Within twenty-four Olympian hours, roughly one week on earth, his heart would be hopelessly lost to the first creature to cross his path. Anteros's eyes were involuntarily drawn back to the lumpy-limbed figure in front of him. He could feel the pull starting already. Hades Balls! He'd imprinted on the hideous creature with the rubbery feet and runny nose. A mortal! A groan escaped his pursed lips. Why a mortal and why'd it have to be so damn ugly?

Anteros' heart bashed up against his chest wall and the last of his fog cleared. Zeus's beard, they might as well have condemned him to eternal torture in the lowest levels of Tartarus as this.

He was doomed. With the use of a golden arrow, not only was his heart forfeit, his soul would soon be irrevocably tied to hers. When she died, she'd take him with her.

Not only had they ruined his life, they'd killed him by robbing him of his immortality!

Anteros couldn't decide which was worse, the burning in his heart from the arrow's path, the hole in it from the enormity of his family's betrayal, or the fact he would never know a moment's freedom from the monstrous ice encased mortal currently hoping from one foot to the other screeching like a banshee as she hovered over him.

"Hey Mister? I'm sorry, really. Oh gosh, what can I do? Can I help you up maybe? Do you need a doctor? Or is there someone else I can call?"

The concern in her eyes pulled on his heart strings and, to his horror, other things as well. Stupid arrow was working all right.

"Who are you? Can you tell me your name?"

Uh, tell her his name? Come to think of it, probably not. Hmm, let's see, how did one explain such things to a mortal?

Hello, I'm a pissed off god who's been shot with the equivalent of a super love potion slash aphrodisiac by 'Stupid Cupid' and you, you lucky thing, are now the target of my every superhuman desire. Something, by the way, that will build in potency to a point I'll no longer be able to resist and will very likely jump all over you. Which really isn't working for me because the second I do, the arrow's magic will pierce you too - lovely little golden bugger that it is - and you'll fall for me against your will. In turn, my immortality goes up in smoke and I'll die the second you do.

Oh and since you asked, my name is Anteros, God of Love Returned, Dread Avenger of Unrequited Love, brother of Eros and son of Aphrodite and Ares. Let's have sex right now. How do you like me so far?

Oh, yeah, that should go over real well.

For more information on other Bandit Creek Tales,
visit www.banditcreekbooks.com

Authors Note:

Although I grew up around the sport of Chuckwagon racing and believe I've stayed true to the spirit and excitement inherent in it, I in no way claim to be an expert, or that the details contained within the confines of this book are to be considered a completely factual representation.

I've taken some liberties with the actual mechanics and terminology of the sport of Chuckwagon racing in the interest of brevity and to create an exciting ride for the story's hero.

Author's Shameless Request:

If you enjoyed this book, please consider posting a review on Amazon or Goodreads - if you didn't - well, then it'll be our little secret.
Just kidding - all honest reviews are welcome and appreciated always.

Again, thank you, Dear Reader I hope you had as much fun reading Chase and Jenna's *Wild* romantic ride as I did writing it. ☺

Links:

I do encourage anyone interested in the real world of Chuckwagon Racing, to check out **www.halfmileofhell.com**, where you'll find information on everything from its history to today's rules and standings. There are also links to current participants and profiles on the stars of the past, both of the two and four legged variety.

For more information on the Calgary Stampede, check out **www.calgarystampede.com**

For details about the Western Art Show click on **www.westernshowcase.com**

And if, like me, you are concerned about the state of the few remaining Wild Mustangs and would like to learn more, in Southern Alberta, check out the Wild Horses Society of Alberta at **www.northernhorse.com/wildhorses.**

Or I suggest looking up 'wild mustang' on the internet for information on individual herds, along with adoption and management efforts in your local area. Please add your voice for the sake of their preservation.

Author Bio: Kymber Morgan

Kymber Morgan lives in the shadow of the Rocky Mountains in the heart of cowboy country and grew up with her own link to mythology through a family legend involving the Fae, giving her tons of fodder to draw on when crafting her stories.

Kymber writes both contemporary and paranormal romance and loves nothing better than giving life to the voices in her head. Whether they belong to a nummy hunk-a-faery and the feisty heroine who charmed him, a to-die-for cowboy and the gal who roped him, or a gorgeous Greek God and the mortal who claimed him, they all find a home on the page with her.

Come join the fun at www.kymbermorgan.com, follow her on twitter @kymbermorgan or check out her author page www.facebook.com/KymberMorganAuthor because with friends like these, you never know who else may be dropping by. Or you can email her at author@kymbermorgan.com. She loves to hear from her readers.

Made in the USA
San Bernardino, CA
12 April 2017